THE DAY I MET FREEDOM

I0552240

MIRIKA MAYO CORNELIUS

Author of the bestselling Curse the Cotton, An Evil Was Born and The Secret Novel Collection

THE DAY I MET FREEDOM

THE DAY I MET FREEDOM

ISBN-13: 978-1-946870-08-7
Copyright © Mirika Mayo Cornelius, June 2019

An Akirim Press Publishing
Book Cover by Akirim Press/Mirika Mayo Cornelius
www.akirimpress.com

THE DAY I MET FREEDOM

Acknowledgements

I first and always thank God for the giving of his Son, Jesus, to save me, and I acknowledge and confess that without Him, I have and am nothing.

I love you, son. Forever I love you, and thank you.

mirikacornelius.com

This book is dedicated to my forefathers and mothers who survived, fought and died in America. I will never forget you.

THE DAY I MET FREEDOM

THE DAY I MET FREEDOM

Imagine meeting Freedom for the first time, and it brings you the most sorrow, pain and joy of your entire life. This is the story of Wani, Iney and Oseen who would do anything for Freedom, but would Freedom do anything for them and at what cost?

Table of Contents

THE DAY I MET FREEDOM

INTRODUCTION

"The Real Slave"

Why call me a slave when you worse off than
me?
Lookin' down on me like I'm the one rapin'
lil children, lyin' on God, and livin' off the
ground your own hands soaked in innocent
blood.

Why you lookin' at me like I'm somebody to
despise when it's you who tanglin' up people
with ropes on they necks so you can laugh,
dance, party, and watch as they struggle to
breathe and die?

And you lookin' down on me, like I'm the
one who need to be feared and fixed, like I'm
the one who need to be taught better, when
my hands ain't never whipped a baby's skin
off her back.
My hands never cut men's manhoods from
they bodies as they hung from trees or
drowned a many sodomized ladies in the
sorrowful seas.

Yeah, you got everybody fooled, like we
crazy, the ones you call slave, but I'd rather
have my soul draped in innocence and love
than covered in hate and hell like you as I lay
in my grave.

You call me a slave only 'cause of my body,
and that's alright by me, but I'ma call you a
slave 'cause your evil, rotten soul ain't gonna
never be
FREE.

THE DAY I MET FREEDOM

I've been dead now for near 'bout some centuries I reckon, but I need to tell my story to you because I never got a chance to do it. Sometimes, my soul quakes even though I'm dead. I don't know if a soul is supposed to do that at times, but mine does, especially when people want to forget about me. People think that's all I is, is dead, but they forget 'bout the inside part of me. I can't rest good when my own people forget 'bout me, or don't want me no mo' 'cause this grave swallowed what they call me…a slave. I was still a person one time with feelings and things I woulda' liked to do, no matter how they say. It was hard enough trying to remember who I was myself, so I need people to remember me, remember who I was and things, remember that I liked to smile if I could and liked to even dance if that was a possibility. I want people to know that I wasn't no animal, but I that I felt feelings just like you feel today, 'cept I was trapped inside a jail between oceans, and even lakes, rivers and streams, between a place that took me but really didn't want me and another place where it seemed like half of 'em turned against me and forgot about me...us. Water on all sides of me. We was all trapped and on our own. Sometimes, them oceans was the worse thing ever made to me because it kept me from leaving but drew me to dying. Kept me from leaving... leaving from the land that hated me so much 'til I reckoned I was the enemy of it, that I did something wrong to it when I didn't. All I did was work for it, help it grow and be hated for it. Who said dark skin was a bad thing and when?

Anyhow, I was 'round about twenty five years old, and my mama had done slipped away into glory already, and my papa was in the fields. Me, I was with Massah Duncan. He was young and hot headed, the son of his papa as I ever did see. He had me out there in them woods near evening time doing whatever he wanted with me. He did whatever, too. I had to take it, and I hurt so bad, in my body and in my heart, so bad that I felt like an animal. While we were out there in them woods, I saw something that I'd never seen a day in my life. I saw Freedom. I tell you that I ain't never seen something so beautiful in all my days on top of the earth. Never.

"Turn over."

He was done. The whole time he was pushing me forward, on me like a dog on another dog, I kept looking North. The sun was going down, so there were glimmers of sunlight that peeked through the trees. I focused on the light. It was the only pretty thing left of the day, so I imagined myself playing in it, walking on the rays so I could block out the darkness that happened to me all the time. Everybody knew Massah Duncan was rapin' me every week, whenever he wanted. He'd done started it when I was eleven, and kept doing it. I used to fight back, but he would hit me, beat me 'til I couldn't stand up, and I had to lay down. My mama's cries for me bruised me on the inside worse than any whip or fist could do to my physical body though. Once, my body was so tired of the pain that when it laid down on the dirty ground, my fingernails tried to dig my own grave. I was willin' to lay down in it alive so I could die as the warm dirt covered my wounds. It was after he hurt me that he then completed his mission. Sometimes, he would do it once, and other times he would do it multiple times, even while I was bloody and all. I was passed down to him as a gift from his father to use me in that way. It made him happy to hurt his gift. I was a present he could hurt. After, when my mama was living, she would feed me roots so I would lose what might come forth from me later.

His daddy had two of what he called concubines who looked like me, and his wife turned a blind eye. She knew though, and she hated all us for it, like it was our fault her husband was the pure devil. He was born that way. I suspected she was born to look away from his evil ways and pretend she saw some good where there was none.

As for me, no other man wanted me as I grew into a lady. It wasn't because the flesh of my back looked like mountains with streams of blood draining down the cracks half of the time because half of their backs had the same streams and mountains as mine did. We would all get whipped for fun sometimes, especially when Massah Duncan was angry at something. He would hold the whip in his hand and just hit whoever he felt like hittin' once or twice. We all got it. But no, men not touching me or desiring me as I got older wasn't because of how I looked. It was because until Massah Duncan relieved me to myself, I couldn't have myself to marry any man. No one could show me love ...openly. I didn't submit to him out of fear of him nor for myself. Like I said about my mama's screams, I submitted for my mama. She couldn't bear either one, the rapin' of me or the whippings, but it was the whippings that was the visible thing. That was when I could hear her screams like it was happening to her. I just started taking the rape, so I wouldn't kill mama. She would just rock and wait. She used to stop rocking when I walked back in the cabin. Then, she would wash me and hold me all night as I cried. The next days later, we would start all over. Although I didn't want her to die, she died anyway, and that was when I started to feel like it was me that was her weakness. If I died she would hurt. If I lived, she would hurt. I had to been done hurt her heart so much on both sides that she couldn't keep from dyin'. She didn't wake up that day, and the tears was still on her face when I got back. It was a day Massah took me again. That made her cry to death. Papa was holdin' her when I got there.

I turned over like he said. "Yessir." I didn't look back at him when I finally did turn over. That was the only thing I could do to spite him after he had his way with me. He was the ugliest looking white man on the plantations for miles. His face looked like something went wrong with it, and he knew it. He would punch my face to make it look just as ugly as his, and he used to put out his pipe ashes into my wounds. He did that up until his daddy saw my burning face. His words to his son were *"How you expect to even want to have her if she look like a monster… like you? Any place you got to look at shouldn't be all burned up like that? She dark enough, ain't it?"* That's the reason why he started turning me over, so he wouldn't have to look at me and the wounds he caused. Each time he touched me in that way, vomit would pour from my mouth. When he was done, there would be enough of it to throw back in his face, but I never threw it. I wished I did. I felt like my vomit was whatever nasty demon sap he was putting in me. I couldn't vomit on my back, so being on my stomach made it easier to empty myself, make myself feel clean on the inside. He heard me heaving each time, but he didn't care. Sometimes, I wanted to vomit my whole soul out, but it wouldn't leave. I didn't know what it was clinging to.

"Stay here."

I hated those words. I'd tried to run away from it all plenty times, twice I was caught and whipped until I couldn't walk for three whole days. That was when my papa got hit so many times over his head that all he ended up good for was picking cotton. They cut out his tongue afterwards and made him dumb. He did it for me. I asked him not to go after Massah Duncan for nearly killin' me, but when he caught a glimpse of me laying there half dead, that was supposed to be Massah Duncan's last time living. Papa was gonna kill Master Duncan, and he would have if it wasn't for Big Massah Duncan's coming to rescue him. He took my papa by the throat until he passed out. When he woke up, he beat him in his face until he passed out again. I thought he was gonna kill him. Big Massah Duncan didn't like what he called a dead slave. He liked to keep what he considered his property for as long as he could, so instead of too many hangings, he would chain us up when we got caught doing whatever he didn't want us to do. Everybody had to watch when the torture was happening. He chose my daddy's tongue to cut out for what he said was a crime against a white man, his only son. He dared anyone to cry or they were next. I didn't cry. My mama passed out, but I didn't cry. No, I shole didn't cry, but it cut my spirit so much that I fell to my knees, but I didn't cry because my papa, before his tongue was cut out shouted at me, *Don't cry, Wani!*

I knew why he told me that, why he chose those words as his last ones. It would hurt him more than his own tongue being out if he had to watch mine being cut out the same. My papa was a singing man. He had the best voice on the plantation, and that was why Big Massah Duncan took his words from him. Taking his legs or his hand wouldn't have mattered much and would have hurt Big Massah Duncan in the long run. It was my papa's tongue that mattered. My papa never been the same since. He was beat in the head, too. He would just stand up and sit down, no words, no strength…just stare at me. Just stared, like he was sorry, like he wasn't settled no more like he used to be.

It was from that day, the day that my papa went quiet, that I was trapped because Big Massah Duncan had already gotten into my heart with pain and my head with my bleeding papa. Just them two things became stronger than the ocean that kept me trapped. I only had one family, and that was more than most had around me. All I needed to keep me obedient was that vision of my papa gettin' his tongue cut from him after trying to protect me from all the raping and beatings they used to keep me in line. Big

23

Massah Duncan was gonna hurt my family all the day long if I'd done another thing against him. That was the last time I heard my papa call my name. Soon after that, my stomach started growing. I had my first baby. Massah Duncan made her his slave, too, especially when he saw her. She wasn't no mulatto like the kind he was used to seeing. No. My baby wasn't that light. She was growin' brown too fast… and too much. She wasn't as dark as me though, so he was confused. She was gonna be his slave anyway, but he was gonna take more mercy on her because she had his blood running through her veins, I supposed. He had a right to be confused because she wasn't his baby. I didn't ever say whose it was to him. That was the secret man I loved and that loved me back. He was to stay secret, even to my own child, 'less Massah Duncan kill him or sell him off. It was a risk for a man to love me openly, so it was only one time. It happened one time. That was the first time I felt soft touches and warm, dark skin on my own. I forbade him for coming around me anymore because I loved him, and he loved me and soon us. I didn't

24

take the roots those weeks. That baby I was gonna keep, and that growth in my stomach was gonna be my rest.

Anyhow, after Massah Duncan went off to do his hunting, for he liked to hunt after raping me, I stood there like he said. This time, he wasn't hunting for any animals. He was hunting for humans, colored ones like myself. He leveled us lower than the dogs they used to sniff us out and chase us. There was some runaways on the loose for their lives, and Massah Duncan wanted to find 'em. They moved at night, and the evening was setting in.

As he walked away and I stood there in that same spot where he ordered me to stay, I soon enough knew something wasn't the same about the night. The night was finally black, like all the other nights, but I felt something different in the air. The feeling was so different, and as I stared forward, I knew the air was excited about somethin', and it was writin' me messages about what it was hiding all over my skin, in a language that only my people could understand.

I searched closer without even moving from my spot. There was a way the white man didn't know about, and it was how to hear and search with the wind and the leaves. They make a certain type of music all the time, but the music was a different tune that night. It wasn't the same. Something was pausing the song in the wrong places and playin' when it shouldn'tve been playin'. I shut my eyes to concentrate, only to open them one more time, and this time, not even five feet from me, I saw Freedom staring right back at me between the trees. As still as the moon sat in the sky so bright and in between all the bright stars, there she was, and every rip on my body and soul healed up as her dark eyes settled onto me, her face as smooth and beautiful as bronze.

Not being able to help myself, I stepped forward, reaching out, scared to death by the gulfs at the bottom of my eyes that filled with tears. Once again, I knew I couldn't cry because when my mouth parted and quivered, the barrel of a long gun met my breath in mid air. It was her. I choked as the tears fell down my face, not nearly more afraid of that gun than

I was afraid of being a slave for the rest of my life. Pressin' my hand around my mouth to keep chains on my voice, I watched the barrel of the gun sink back into the shadows of the trees, and again, my stomach quaked. I still hadn't yet fixed my clothes back onto my naked body when I began to rock back and forth because I couldn't contain my pleas without moving myself with the pain. I dared not turn around for fear I would alert Massah Duncan, so I kept my eyes on her, not even pulling my torn dress from the ground to cover myself while Freedom looked me stone in my face. She was mighty. She was fearless. She was smart. She was able…but it became clear that she didn't come for me.

I finally took a shallow breath so my life wouldn't pass. Then, I searched beyond the trees that stood tall around Freedom to see if there were more with her. There were two. I wanted to run there and at least touch her, but when I took another step, she stood up and aimed the gun at my forehead.

"Please," I begged quieter than a whisper, but I knew she heard my heart. My legs got weak as I

27

thought about my child and my papa whose only cause in life was to stare back at me. Those thoughts caused me to fall to my knees. "They gonna kill my baby. Please, I need to go back and get my papa, too. Don't leave us, please, I beg you with all my life."

Minutes went by with only silence, and finally, Freedom stepped out. She was calmer than any runaway fugitive I'd ever seen, and as she walked toward me, she continued to lower herself until she was on her knees and inches away from my broken, naked body. The tears that fell to my body fled to meet her clothes with so hard a pounding that she reached around my mangled soul and hugged it so powerfully that it gave me the relief I needed for the first time in my life. My arms hugged her like she was my own mother.

"I can't take no babies. He also got your scent, so I can't take you either." Her eyes moved to where my clothes lay, and then, she let me go. The air that traveled in between us felt like it was the whip itself opening up my already screamin' pores. That was my last time holding Freedom. I watched her slowly back away, aiming her gun, no longer at me, but in the direction of Massah Duncan. When the leaves came to take her from the openness, I watched her gun drop from view.

I stood back up and put on my dress. Then, I looked down at my feet and hands. They seemed to be loose just like Freedom's, but they were really in the largest chains ever made, that bond between my baby and me. Freedom started to seem so small when I compared it to the 'tachment I had to my child. If Freedom couldn't take my baby, I would have to, so I ran. I left Freedom right where she was, and I ran my hardest because I knew if I could run fast enough, I could feel Freedom through the woods again, even if she left before I got back. Massah Duncan would be out there, sure enough, but I would watch…watch until I saw him coming from out those woods, and I would set off again. I knew in what direction Freedom was headed, and I only had a short time to get there with my own. She told me no, but now that I'd done touched her, I knew Freedom was real. She was able to be felt and held. She was real. It was real.

"Papa. Papa, get up and get everything in your pockets. Put your shoes on and come on, Papa. Keep quiet, no moaning. Gimme my baby. I got to wrap her tight so she hush." He grabbed my wrist, stopping me from my dying need for us to leave. "Papa, let go. We got to go. I saw her…" I panted, yanking my arm trying to get away from his grip, but I wasn't strong enough to break free. "Papa, let go!" He wouldn't stop, and as I started to fuss with him again, I watched tears roll from his face. Then, he looked down at his hand as it held me in place. As I stopped fighting and looked him in his eyes, he suddenly let me go. I then understood what he was trying to tell me. He nodded his head and kissed me on my forehead while stroking my daughter on her cheek. He knew he would hold me back, so he was setting me free to run... without him.

We embraced for as long as we could, and when it was all over, he shoved me out the door. He followed me before stopping at the spot where Massah Duncan normally entered back onto the plantation. I ran in the opposite direction with my baby wrapped onto my side so that if she cried, I could cover her mouth or feed her quickly. It was just me and her. I knew what my papa was gonna do. He was gonna complete that same something he tried to do before they made him speechless just so I could survive and get what was owed to me and mine.

As I ran, I kept stopping and looking back, my heart torn for knowing that papa was giving his life for mine, just to make the search for me slow and confused so I could get away. I loved my papa dearly and didn't want him to do it, but I also understood why he needed me and my baby free. To him, that was making him live just like savin' my baby was making me live. While runnin', I also thought about my love who lived near. I wanted to make a turn to stop off and tell him, but I couldn't. I had to make it back to that place where Freedom was so my papa's life, and maybe even soon to be death, wouldn't be in vain. We was meant to live and die for something, and this was our something – Freedom.

"Wani! Wani! Gal, get back here now!" he shouted. "You're asking for a good one this time, the worst one yet, and this time, I just might let you die. Wani!" he shouted, ripping through the limbs of trees with the barrel of his gun. The sound of his voice was a call for slave blood, and as he called my name again and again, suddenly, the sound of the call was cut short. He didn't even get my full name out, and my name wasn't that long. I stopped everything, even stopped breathing, just to listen to the trees. Then, I started breathing heavier, excited for papa, as I listened to the wind again. It carried no sound for seconds until there it was. It wasn't the sound of gunfire. It was the sound of death, the sound of a white man's death. It was always quiet, not loud like a Negro's dying. There was never any weeping, not from the muts or the flying animals, when a white man died. Nothing was sad, and nothing wailed. I knew it wasn't my papa's death because when we had to kill, we didn't make noise, no noise of guns or whips. We killed quiet. Negro men like my papa knew how to stalk and kill with their bare hands, and even though I heard that silent sound of white death, I also heard joy in the leaves. Those same leaves that watched what went on all my life, fanning us while the limbs of trees was left with the burden of holding us kind of folks up with knotted ropes because the whites thought it was funny. Those same trees brought me the strength of my papa by waving his song of victory to me. He couldn't sing no more, but the same way they took his words, he was gonna take theirs, not just Massah Duncan's son, but Big Massah Duncan's himself. The leaves clapped a certain tune for one evil Massah down, but the clapping didn't stop. They kept clapping, and then came my sorrow.

"Papa," I cried softly as my body fell against the ground, hoping that the leaves would carry my message back to him. "Please, come now. That's enough. Just come now." Although I asked, I knew he wasn't going to come. The earthquake beneath my knees told me he was stomping toward the big house. That was how I knew he wasn't coming. He had two men to kill, so it wasn't over. Either way, I couldn't stay. Not anymore. I stood up from that quaking ground, but it wasn't long before I heard a lone gunshot and then another. The leaves sent me the message. The death was loud, and the dogs started howlin' and the birds left from their nests in the middle of night. My papa died. I ran harder than I'd ever run before. My heart more broken than it ever been before because I knew papa was gone, and me and my baby was all alone.

CHOOSE THE STORY'S PATH:

THE DAY I GOT FREEDOM (Go to page 29)

THE DAY I SAW FREEDOM BURN (Go to page 42)

THE DAY I GOT FREEDOM

My feet never ran as fast as they did that day. The branches of the trees shoved me faster and faster, and each time I looked back to see if anyone was behind me, the trees covered up my path to keep those eyes of the white man from seein' me. But I heard the dogs. They didn't need eyes. They could smell me.

"Help me, Freedom. Please, I ain't never done nothing to offend you, so please help me."

My ankles bled. I felt the sores drainin' my blood like an old, wet rag rang out water. I was used to being whipped, so the taps from the switches didn't slow me down, and the blood didn't make me slip and fall. Freedom kept me runnin'. I wasn't never gonna fall until I got to her, me and my baby.

The barking of the dogs got louder and louder, so my feet pounded the ground quicker and harder. I didn't know which way to turn or which way to go after a certain point, so I just kept runnin' away. Away was where I was supposed to go. That place was everywhere but there.

"Mama not gonna let 'em do you like they did me. We both gonna die runnin' if we have to, so grow them legs faster. You can't stay a baby no more. You got to grow on our way to Freedom. You hear me? You can't be a baby, and I can't hold you long. You have to grow fast." I told her, holdin' her tight as I leaped across the ground like a horse.

My heart hurt from the pain it got from being too tired, but I wasn't gonna stop. I'd rather my heart just stop beatin' than me stop runnin'. Tears rolled down my face, but I imagined it was just water to drink to keep me going. The dogs were closin' in on me, and Freedom was nowhere in my sight. Not anywhere. It was dark. There was no light. Then, it bit me, but I didn't fall.

Instead of screamin', I took all that pain and kicked it while it chewed on my leg. My arms was full of my baby while I leaned on a tree. I wasn't never gonna let her go, so I kept kickin' that dog 'til he let me go, and I stomped him to death or near it. Then, another came runnin', and he jumped right on me, too close to bitin' my baby, so I knocked it from me. It came back, and I bit it 'til I took a whole piece of meat from his body as I fell to the bloody ground. That dog screamed louder than me. Wasn't no teeth marks harder than no whip, harder than no rape, and harder than the pain of my papa dyin'. Wasn't no pain harder than not bein' free.

As I got back on my two feet, it felt like my own legs were fighting against me, and then a familiar pain hit my back that tore me to the ground.

"Where you goin', gal? You ain't got no clue where you goin' do you? A dog got more sense than a nigger…and you takin' my property with you, I see."

I squeezed my child tight as they yanked me up from my knees, and as they did, I saw the rope. It was thick and long, long enough to drape across any one of the limbs that reached for me in sadness. As I studied the rope, every word that them whites was

37

sayin' to me fell silent to the death of my own self. There wasn't no tears on my face no more, and my baby was screamin'. That was the only sound I heard. It was the first time I didn't want to comfort her. The sound of her loud cryin' comforted me because I soon wasn't gonna hear it no more. That rope was gonna take my memories away.

Each time the whites came for me, I wrestled my baby away from 'em. They kept touchin' her, pokin' her, and yankin' at her legs, laughin' at me tryin' to protect her with all the might I had. Then, I heard the rope slither on the limb of a tree. I turned around to see it, the place where my feet would leave the earth before my spirit. Finally, one of them whites knocked me down while Big Massah Duncan watched. Next thing I felt was the noose from that long rope goin' 'round my head and tightening on my neck.

I rushed to my feet so I could stay with my baby a little while longer as they pulled the rope, but then, her cry was interrupted by my struggle to breathe. My toes lifted from the ground. One of my arms grabbed for the rope that was tearing through the skin at my throat. I tried to pull it down some, but it gave me only a little bit of extra time before my other arm that was holdin' my baby started gettin' weak. It was before my eyes shut from being too weak against the fight that death was bringing 'em, I watched Big Massah Duncan walk up and take my only child from my arm. At first, he took her away easy, like he cared. I thought he would, being that he thought there was a chance that my baby was his grand, but suddenly, all that easiness went away.

"Leave her," he ordered them in a rage, and then he shouted at me. "Your baby gonna make me plenty more! Plenty more! Your papa killed my boy! My son! I seen him out there…he ain't never been worth a nothin', but he was still mine! Now you die, just like I'ma go back there and lift your dead papa up from the front of my house. I watched him murder my boy from the house. I saw it! He was callin' for you, and I looked out. It was your papa!" He walked up to me, my baby still crying and said, "I met that papa of yours eye to eye when I got to my porch with my gun. That old nigger thought he could take a bullet 'cause he didn't stop comin' at me, and I shot your old papa dead." He smiled. "They gonna pass by you everyday and know, and even this thing here," he shouted, shoving my baby toward the sky, "She gonna see your body hangin' right there as she grows. I'ma bring her back here tomorrow and the next day and the next so she can see the crows take you away piece by piece."

They walked away, laughin' and tossin' my baby back and forth like she was a ball, and while they did that, my body shook as I struggled to live and get her back. It was then, that I suddenly felt Freedom once again, even though this time, I couldn't see her. My toes felt movement underneath me, and my feet stood on something solid, like ground again, and all the pressure from the rope eased up off my throat. I choked back air to stay alive.

"Keep quiet! Be still as you can, Joseph," she said to the person underneath my feet. "Hold her good and still. Sire, get here and catch her when she drop. Keep your eyes forward 'til they gone." She then spoke to me. "Keep quiet there, chile, and don't you cry. I know you know how to do that. We all do."

My eyesight came back, and my chest filled back up with the Lord's air. As it did, I opened up my mouth to call for my baby, but a hand went over it, and I fell into a person's arms.

"Good thing you ain't got much size to you. They didn't have to pull you so high, but I'm gonna need for you to shut your mouth. Don't be hollerin' for that baby of yours because she don't understand you no how."

As I choked back new air into my chest and took down water that tasted like it came from a mountain spring, I opened up my eyes again to make sure I wasn't in heaven already. There she was. It was Freedom. It was her, and I didn't have to be ashamed of my tears or my fears anymore. I hugged her so tight.

"Enough huggin'. Take that dress off. We got to stuff it, and put it back on the tree. Hurry now," Freedom ordered, and at once, another started pulling my dress from me and stuffing it with leaves, twigs, branches and other things from our rooted friends. The trees didn't mind. The only thing they always hated was when evil was done on 'em and not good.

After my dress got stuffed with the trees, it was pushed back through that noose and hung back on the tree just like if it was me myself. Then they forced men clothes on me and kept it from fallin' off me with a belt.

"We got to go. Move."

"My baby," I snatched from the one called Sire's hand and fell to the ground. "They got my baby."

"I know they got your baby!" Freedom stood tall over me as I gained the strength to stand back on my own two feet. "You think that child gonna be in the fields where we can go grab her? Huh? You think you can just run up there and get her without a plan?

You think she gettin' whipped because she ain't? She's right down a ways…"

"But that's my baby…"

Freedom stopped talkin' and put her head down beneath the leaves. We all dropped down with her. I saw she was plannin' something.

"I heard three voices," said Sire.

"There was four," I answered. "He got four men, and one of 'em is one of us."

"You got to be bait," Freedom told me. "We all got guns, not many bullets, but we got to get 'em before they reach the big house. You got to go runnin' for 'em when you can't see us anymore. You hear me? Answer me!"

"Yes, yes ma'am. I hear you." Truth was that I heard her loud and clear, except I couldn't see my baby no more. I kept looking through the trees while she was talkin', heard every word, but listening to her kept me from seeing my blood born.

"You go runnin' loud and screamin'. Take the dress outta that noose quick, Sire, and let her put it back on. I ain't riskin' their lives for you twice. Bait 'em right, and we won't miss. Bring 'em back, and we will be waiting in the trees for the right time to strike. If we can't strike, you on your own." She stood up. "I would give my life for my baby, too, but hopefully, ain't nobody givin' they life away tonight 'cept them."

"What about the dogs?" I asked.

"Don't let 'em kill you."

"And if they do?"

"What's your name?"

"Wani."

"I will take lil Wani with me. Put her with some good people who won't let her be no slave."

"But that's not her name."

"So she can remember her mother, if need be. If need be not, you can keep callin' her what you call

44

her because she will still be with you. Sire … Joseph … get into position. When you can't see us, get the attention of them white men, Wani, and do it fast."

My heart beat like it never beat before. Not even runnin' from Big Massah Duncan and them made it beat like this, not this fast. I never called my killers to me before, but I was willin' to call 'em one thousand whole times to kill me for my baby girl. When I didn't hear or see them anymore, I howled like a groanin' wolf for my child and went runnin' forward as much as I could. My voice carried stronger and faster than my sore legs and feet could.

"Gimme my baby! You can't kill me, and I ain't gone let you. Bring me my baby! I'll kill you all for my child! Massah Duncan! You bring her here! She mine, all mine! She'll never be yours…not ever!"

I heard them dogs first. Their barks called at me like they was mad they had to come back. The next thing I heard were them whites runnin', hollerin' back at me. There was a big wind that blew into my sores, and I knew then that the angels of God were with me, whether I lived or died. More than likely I was gonna die. Wind blew harder when death came close. I was ready to fight it. I was gonna get my freedom somehow, and my baby, too.

I balled up my fist and grabbed a branch from the ground with my other hand. I could see them dogs chargin' at me like I wasn't no human being at all, and when one jumped, I knocked it flat down with all the strength I had with that branch. The next one jumped, and I punched it as hard as I could but fell when the other one bit down on my ankle. My papa taught me to bite back, so that was what I done. I bit, hit and kicked and wasn't gonna stop until I heard the gunshots I needed to hear.

My screams woke the dead, and every time the dogs bit me, I felt like arms was gonna pull me down beneath the ground to spare me all the pain. I saw one time when dogs bit up a man to death, but I wasn't gonna die like him. I couldn't die, not 'til I seen my baby safe.

There went the first gunshot, then a second, and then a third. Soon as I looked back up, there was Joseph, stabbin' the dogs from off me with a knife so long it was meant to kill anything living.

"Shhh. Hush now," he said, trying his best to cover my wounds as I cried. "I know it hurt there. That man you used to call Massah, he over there, and we got to get you there. Wrap this 'round you."

"Y'all got 'em all?"

"For right now. More will soon be comin' so we got to shed our scent. Let's go. Hop on." He pat his back, and I inched on slowly due to the bites I had all over me. "You can do it. You done been through worse, like most of us. You strong. You gonna make it. Let's go."

He took off runnin' from underneath my death tree as it waved behind me, and 'fore I knew it, I was lookin' Massah Duncan right in his face while Freedom had my baby locked in her arm, and Sire had Massah Duncan by the throat. Joseph put me down, and just as soon as he did, all the trees seemed

47

like they gathered around, waitin' on what they knew was 'bout to happen. Everything was still.

"Come over here, but don't get your baby from me yet," Freedom said. "Now, you look at him." I looked at him, but to Freedom, I wasn't lookin' at him right so she shouted at me…made me jump clear out my own skin. "I said look at him! Look him in his eyes, and don't you never forget that this is what them eyes look like. Suck it all in, and don't you dare listen to his beggin'," she said as she glared at him, "because he ain't never listened to yours."

I ain't never seen Big Massah Duncan's eyes. Every time he came too close, we looked down. If I saw his eyes, it was from far away, and I never dared to look into 'em too long, so it wasn't in my mind too much at all. Tonight was different. I walked up close to his eyes, just like Freedom told me to do, and it was right then that I took both my hands while my baby stayed crying in Freedom's arm, and I punched all of the blood that I could out of him. I knew he wasn't a dog, but I wanted him to feel like one so I kept hittin' him just like he was an ole dog, one of them dead dogs that he sent to bite me. I wanted him dead, and I wanted to laugh while I was tryin' to kill him like they did me while they was hangin' on that tree, but I couldn't laugh. I was so mad – mad for my papa, mad for myself, and even mad for my baby who they was tossin' and ready to rape like they did me.

"Let it all out. Let it all out on him. I got my gun on him."

I heard Freedom talkin', right behind my ear, and I did just that. I kept on lettin' it all out. I let all my anger out for myself, my mom and papa, and the rest of us.

"Sometimes it take that to move on. You ain't got to kill him though. I will. You can't do it without dreamin' 'bout it, and you need your mind right to raise that free baby you 'bout to have. He so evil he ain't gonna wanna die after the beatin' and stompin' you givin' him anyway because he still think he better than you, but when I put this trigger to his temple, he gonna finally regret the day he been rapin' and beatin' all y'all."

"You stop hittin' me, gal. You can go free! Stop hittin'… look here! I will go write up your free papers myself, right tonight!" he kept callin' until Freedom pulled me by my arm, but his beggin' didn't stop. Then, he spit at Freedom. "It's you, ain't it? We gonna kill you yet! It ain't over, Wani! They gonna find you and your child if you kill me and do worse to her than ever been done to you. You … all of you … I'm your master! You can't kill me." He slammed the ground with his fists as Sire continued to point his gun directly at him.

"It's time to go and run on with Sire and Joseph. Take your baby," she said, handing her to me. "There's more out there waitin'." She turned to look at Big Massah Duncan. "You're about to hear the death of your bondage, Wani, and only hear it, unless you want to look on. Everybody got the choice."

"I wanna see."

"You can see, long as you don't become like them. They like to watch us die. We ain't that breed. I don't kill 'cause I like it. I kill so the ones who find 'em can see that when I come, I come ready to take the chains off, live or die. I ain't becomin' like 'em. I'm settin' my people free 'cause the whites won't. It's a difference."

"Then, I better not look." I turned around. "'Cause I already like it too much. Don't a soul wanna burn in hell like his will...but I can listen as I walk away." Then, I turned back to face him as he held out his hand to me like I was 'bout to reach back and save him from what he 'caused on himself. "As I walk away with *my* free baby, know you ain't never gonna have her like you had me." I spit on the ground he knelt on, and when I turned my head, Freedom started singin' before she blasted his brains out on that ground. I started to look back at his dead body, but I didn't want none of his soul left in me. Instead, I smiled as I limped on fast behind Sire and Joseph to meet up with the others. I ain't need no memory of death to stain my new freedom because Freedom…she volunteered to take it all.

She met up with us later on the next day, her and another. In three weeks, we were on free land. Freedom – she led me there. Harriet … she helped us right nice.

THE END

(Go back to page 41 to choose the other story path)

THE DAY I SAW FREEDOM BURN

No matter how hard I tried, I never made it to Freedom again. The whites burdened one large tree with my body and took my baby away from me while I watched. I died before the rope killed me. I died when they took my baby. I didn't choose to be no slave, not for me nor mine. It kept takin' me somehow and wouldn't let me go. Now, it had my only baby with nobody to teach her, nobody to die for her, and nobody to love her. It was my first time ever wishing she would just die, but she didn't. She was born to be strong because that was her natural way. It was gonna take a whole lot to kill her, and the days was gonna be so long for her that she was gonna wish the sun wouldn't come out no more. Then, she was gonna wonder why her body keep wakin' up to do nothing but work and get beat and then get raped on. That was gonna be my baby's future unless somebody taught her somethin' else, somethin' like what I saw. Freedom.

As they left with my baby, I took my own last breath as I hung there praying that somebody or something, even if it had to be the wind and the trees, teach my baby about Freedom so she know that it is there … somewhere. They listened. The roots of the tree told me everything in whispers as they ate the decay off of my dead body. They told me that she learned about Freedom … but in a burnin' way … not like I wanted her to learn about it, not at all.

THE CHILD'S STORY

I ain't had a mama, and I ain't never had a papa. It was just me since I could remember. I reckon I imagined myself as one of those plants out yonder, not knowing wherefrom I came but just happen to spring up only to end up afraid, scared to death of being chopped down, like I seen the bigger trees that stood all around me.

That's how it felt to be a slave like me that had nobody. I was just stuck, rooted down to a place and wasn't nothing I could do about it much because I didn't know what was over there across the water or under there far beneath the ground. Had feet to walk, but they didn't walk on water. I knew because I tried. Had legs to run, but seem like they stayed on the white man's grass no matter wheres I coulda' run 'cause all the land be their land, the whole thing, and it go for fields and fields.

Yep, I was scared to death of what I seen. Like a tree, I ain't had no choice but to see it, and when I saw it, I didn't know how else to be. I was a little girl then, way far back in the past from where I be buried now. Way far back in the past…but I ain't never told nobody 'bout what I seen as I got older. I kept it in my own head so it wouldn't come to life and get me out there. That been my freedom. It wasn't much, but it was mine. It was mine back when I was on what they called a plantation, and like I say from this grave here, I was a little ole girl. I did know somethin' though. I wasn't a dummy. I just didn't know how I knew I wasn't one.

"What you mean I can't read? I can," I sassed. I never liked when somebody told me somethin' wrong about myself. If I could do somethin', then I could do it.

"Shut up," he said, his mouth slurred from one side like he done been hit by something in it. It never did open up like mine did on both sides, and every time I asked him what it was that happened to his mouth, he just kept the other side of his mouth shut just the same. I never got an answer.

"But…"

"Listen here!" He grabbed me up by my dirty, torn long shirt as I tried to keep it from rising up to show all my underparts. "I ain't tellin' you again." He leaned over in my ear, grindin' his teeth together like he wanted 'em to crush to pieces. "You can't read! You don't go 'round sayin'…"

"Put her down, Oseen," a calm voice said turning the corner. "That girl right there… you ain't tellin' her right." She leaned over next to a bucket of warm water, dipped her palms inside of it, and sipped it up from her hands. "You might be able to do all things, chile, but the one thing you can't do is admit it." She looked over her shoulder. "Can't be tellin' people, not even folks that look like you, because some that look like you on the outside is really *them* on the inside."

"You mean…"

"Shh…" she whispered to calm me down. "Shole is. That's 'xactly what I mean. Now Oseen here don't know 'bout teachin' or tellin' no chile like you nothin', so if you need to find out somethin', you learn it from me. Since the last one died, I'm the oldest lady here, and I ain't that old. Even though I'm not that old, I still knew your mama and how I know she wanted you safe. She was super smart, you know? That was a smart lady right there now."

"I 'member you told me that you knew her, but I don't believe it. It's hard to believe it when…"

"You was a baby. Massah wife kept you in that house up there 'til you was near 'bout three, and

57

then she put you out here with us. She keep you up there with her like you was some healin'," she said, looking quickly at Oseen and then back at me, "or somethin' she needed since her son got killed out there by your grandpa."

"I don't 'member that either. Don't know who my mama is, and don't know who my grandpa is either. Just know y'all…"

"You wasn't meant to 'member. She, Massah wife, she do that to some, keep 'em up there in that house, and you was one. Glad you made it outta there, too. Some children don't. After she put us out here, she don't act like she know us no more. She been stopped havin' children…can't. Couldn't have many children when she could. Only had that one, and I don't believe she liked him one bit no how, but she loved him. Yeah, I'm sure she loved him. Cried like something else out here, like she ain't never been separated from one like they take ours from us."

"Why she ain't like him?"

"Now you keep quiet," Oseen snapped. "Ain't no need to know why. She just didn't," he said, turnin' my way lookin' madder than ever. "She runs her mouth. She too little, and you know it, Ms. Iney. She gonna get us…"

"Back to what we was sayin' though, Lil Wani."

"My name Wani," I whined. "Don't put that *lil* in front of my name. Everybody do that, and I'm not little…*and* I can read."

"I put the *lil* there because you named after your mama. She was Wani when she came here and when she died. I don't want you to die like her so soon, so if you wanna live, I need you to deny you can read, even small words. If somebody try to force you to read, you read it wrong. Put your finger under the word and read it wrong. If you don't, then I guess you just tired."

"Tired of what?"

"Tired of livin'."

"But I don't know how I know…" I whispered. "Like my letters is O and F, and that makes *of*."

"Chile, I know ya' can read." She flicked her eyes up at Oseen. "'Cause I can, too."

"Ain't it 'bout time to go to sleep? We got more work in the morning," Oseen frowned. "Go on to bed, Lil Wani."

Because he was so mad, that was what I did. I left Ms. Iney, and I went on to my side of the floor and went to sleep, rememberin' the words that I know. I didn't tell them that I found a sheet of paper with that word on it. It had many words on it, and I found it when I was diggin' around about in the dirt close to the cabin. Before somebody saw me, I put it back, pushed the dirt over it and left it there. I figured somebody wanted it hid. I was glad I put it back, too, because if Oseen found out about it as mad as he was with me, I woulda' shole nuff got slapped on my behind, and his hands was bigger than my whole face so that wouldn'ta been good, so I shut up. I shut up just like they told me to … because I still wanted to live and read at the same time because when I thought about, I didn't never see a dead person readin' no how.

"Get out here!" shouted a voice so loud it seemed like it shook the cabin boards. It was that same white man's voice that never sounded nice at all. He always was mad about us. Always. It was Massah. That was his first name. His last name was Duncan. Massah Duncan. "Get out here now!"

It was still nighttime, and everybody 'round me jumped up like it was a fire or a rain cloud on the low ground suckin' everything up. When I saw 'em jump up, I did, too. That was what I always did. I followed what they did, the older ones. That was how I found my way. They taught me everything on how to act, but everything else after that, I just know somehow.

"What's wrong?" Five other people in the hut were scooting around like they were in trouble, all nervous like they could see the dead. One of them finally yanked me from all my staring and talking and shoved me outside where everyone else was already standing. It was just about middle of the season when the leaves start changing colors, but something was happening that made the night feel hotter than what it shoulda' been. There was a fire brewing close by, and I could even taste the smoke.

I pushed my way through the small group of us out there and hid myself at the leg of the tall boy who would play with me all the time in the fields when he was supposed to be workin'. His name was James. He didn't have a last name, just like me. They said our last names we had was all Duncan, 'cause we were his property. They said that wasn't the true last name though. Later, I said I was gonna give myself a last name because I heard other people talkin' 'bout doing the same thing when they got free because it was proper for people to have a last name, and I wanted to be proper. Some said they was gonna stay Duncans like Massah Duncan, and other people say they was gonna make a name from another name. Me, I knew I was gonna take another name other than Duncan when I got to this free everybody talked about because I didn't like him too much. First though, I had to find out what free was and if it was gonna make me act like them whites. I didn't wanna treat me like they treat me and the folks who look like me. If that was what free was, I didn't want no parts of it. It was bad. I never seen a free person that looked like me before, but I knew it was what everybody like me wanted, and it was to be had some way. Wonder how the whites got it?

My hands felt a whole bunch of fast movements where I was holding on, like a leaf in the wind. It was James. He was shaking something bad. There wasn't a part of his body that wasn't. I looked up to the other side of me and saw Ms. Iney standing next to me, and her face was stiff as a piece of wood. She reached over and took James by the hand, and he jumped from his skin at her touch, eyes big like an owl's. I pulled his leg, and he looked down at me like he didn't even know who I was. It was like he seen a ghost inside me, but when that white man Massah Duncan started talkin' again, his eyes left me faster than they came. I knew then something was wronger than it ever was. Ms. Iney didn't let go of James's hand, and when I looked back around through the small crowd, I saw Oseen standing hunched over at the back, his face mad as could be. His head was movin' back and forth like he was about to jump and kill. That was when I got scared. He looked like he could eat one of them white folks whole, raw and whole, and like it. That's how mad he looked.

"Somebody's getting hung tonight," Massah Duncan said with a deep breath. "Gettin' burned on a stake. You already know that. Ain't nothing you can do about it, so don't try. Any of you run to the right or to your left, you die. It'll be real easy, so don't try it. Bullets and whips with ropes, along with the dogs, are waiting on you. There may be more of you than there is me and my overseers, but I got more rounds than you got legs, much less good ones, ain't it now? You know I hate to kill my property because that's a terrible waste of my money, but a terrible offense is just that. It's unforgettable. Now, one of you have to tell me who wrote these here directions, and wrote it in good plain white folks English, too!" He threw a balled up piece of paper at our feet. "Whoever wrote it can not only write but read…and that means death.

We found it right over yonder…showin' itself through the dirt there by that hut while you sleep. Now, I say, whose is it?"

At that moment, James tugged away from Ms. Iney hard, attempting to break free from her grasp, but she tugged back.

"Shhh! You ain't gonna die today, James," Ms. Iney said under her breath.

"Let me go," he cried softly, all the fear in the world coming from each word.

"No. Now, you hush." She turned to him and a tear went across her cheek, then she looked down at me with a smile. After that, she looked back up at James. "I'm going for you, baby. You remember them directions next time. Use your head to remember, not your skill. That way can't nobody see your secret. Watch Lil Wani, you hear, you and Oseen. The other men here, they too hurt or getting too old. That's how Massah Duncan like it, so there ain't a threat. Teach her the best you can. Protect these ladies how you can. You will soon be a man, and folks will need you to keep your head. Put away fear. Show the ones comin' up." She then shoved his hand to the side and stepped forward into the darkness toward Massah Duncan.

"No, no!" another voice rang out. "It's not my sister. Ain't no way, Massah. She can't read nor much as write, sir. What she know about doing something with paper but what you tell her to do with it? Please," she begged. "Her mind ain't right…it must not be, sir," she pleaded from the other end of the crowd. "Iney, what you doin'? Stop it!"

"Hold that gal there back," Massah Duncan told the overseers against the woman who was beggin' and pleadin' for her sister's life. I never seen anything like that, and I was scared because everybody else was scared. But more than that though, I knew 'bout that paper Massah was talkin' about. I thought I buried it back, but they found it. My heart got sad then because I remembered what Ms. Iney told me just before I went to bed about reading and wantin' to live. I knew somebody wasn't gonna live now 'cause of me.

"Massah," Ms. Iney spoke as she turned away from her screaming sister. "I know who it was who wrote them there directions on that paper. You looking at her right here in front of you."

"Iney, you been my property for over twenty, thirty years now," he gloated. "I know more about you than some of my own kind. Ain't a reading and writing bone in your body, so that means one thing – you're protecting somebody that needs no protecting," he smiled. "That's highly commendable of you, wantin' to stand up for others, but it ain't you, and I won't let you."

"Yes sir, I been working your land for over twenty long years. Twenty-eight years to be exact," she paused, "because I know how to count, too. All that time, you never asked me if I could read or write. You just said I shouldn't do it 'less I die, so I suppose this day I'll tell you that I read and I write, so I suppose I die tonight…sir. I ain't protectin' nobody out here, not even myself."

"No! She lyin, sir. She ain't never read nothing a day in her life! Test her," her sister shouted and fought against an overseer who had her by both her arms and pinned to the ground. "Prove her that way. I tell you she ain't never read nothing … never! She protectin' somebody out here, and y'all gonna let my only sister here on this land die? The only family I got? Massah, she can't read! Sell her," she begged. "Sell her. Don't kill her off a lie."

Massah Duncan and everybody else listened to her beg and plead until she could barely breathe a lick of air. She was fightin' and faintin' all at the same time. At that time, I figured out that it was James who musta wrote it, but it was me who didn't bury it back right and Ms. Iney who was gonna pay for it all. I thought James would have moved to save her life, but he didn't. He just stood there, crying and shaking like a leaf in high wind. He wasn't no man yet, but he was scared-er than I was myself. I thought my legs wasn't gonna be able to move to help Ms. Iney, but when I thought about Ms. Iney dyin' though, I got scared-er than my first scared. I didn't want Ms. Iney to die. Then it happened. I just ran out. Left James standin' right there.

"Ms. Iney!" I saw somebody reach for me, but they missed me, and when I got to her leg, I held it tight. "Ms. Iney, don't say that. I didn't mean to…" She immediately reached around and grabbed my cheeks so tight that I thought my own jaws would pop and my teeth would fall out it hurt so bad.

"Go back over there," her voice trembled in my ear, "and teach somebody else what you know in secret plus what I tell you. I'm savin' us all. Bye, chile. I'mma die just fine." Then she shoved me down like she was one of them overseers herself, like she hated me…but she didn't. There were tears in her eyes when she looked at me, but I watched her wipe them dry before she turned back to him.

"Go bring me some of that flame there," he ordered one of his overseers as he shot a mean look at who only looked to be a calm Ms. Iney. She wasn't calm though. I could tell, as some of the others like me drug me back to where they were, that she was just tired because her eyelids hung low and her breathing wasn't like someone who was alive anymore. She wanted to die. I knew she really wanted to die because she told on herself, and it wasn't even her time.

The overseer put some of the flame on the edge of a large piece of wood and walked it back over to Massah Duncan who had already marched that same sheet of paper that I had found over to Ms. Iney, shoving it in her face. Before the flame was held over the paper for light, Ms. Iney spoke.

"I don't need that flame. I can see just fine."

At those words, he punched her in the face, 'cause she wasn't supposed to say that to him like she did. She fell at his feet, but she quickly turned her head from his feet, though, refusing to show him any signs of worship by being down there at his feet. She only worshipped the Lord. She said she was one of the ones with the whole Bible, and she had already read it. Said she was one of the little bit of us who seen a whole one, not one with parts missin' that the whites didn't want us to read. Ms. Iney would always call Massah Duncan the rotten devil. Said if the devil had a face, it was his and most all that look like him.

"Well, since you can see just fine, you make me a liar by reading this paper here! If you so much as read one word, you die tonight. You wrote these here directions?"

"Yes sir," she said with blood dripping from her mouth. "I said I wrote those directions, and you found 'em in just enough time before I shared them freedom directions with the rest of 'em, too." She cut her eyes over to her wailing sister and then at James before speaking back at Massah Duncan. "You ain't a liar, Massah. But I tell you what you is though. You a fool…a fool to think I'm this here old and can't read nothin'." He struck her again, but in her anguish she pushed herself to speak once more. "The first word on that paper is Freedom, and the second word on it is route. R-O-U-T-E…" she proudly spelled it out with a big ole smirk on her bloody face, forgettin' about all the laws Massah Duncan and anybody else had over her ever in her life. She spelled that word out, one that I didn't yet know, right in a white man's face.

71

Massah Duncan's face grew hard and angry, and he shouted, "Hang her and burn her body all night long! None of you better sleep." He swore curses at all us with dark skin who was standing there watching. It had to be about twenty of us and that included the children. "You will watch until she is nothing but dirty ash right along with this here paper!"

Suddenly, Ms. Iney started talkin' again, "Go down by the river, jump the moon on the tip and the slide down the mountain 'til it breaks!" she shouted before being hit across the head and a rope tightened at her throat. She still struggled to tell the road to freedom as she knew some there were trained to remember, even through terror. "Follow the poison…she's there! She's there. Run and run fast. Remember the break at the bottom of the mountain! Follow the poison! There be healin' on the other side!"

"Shutup! Just set her on fire now! Do it now," Massah Duncan rushed because the words she was shoutin' musta' been true, and he wanted to shut her up as soon as he could. None of us had ever been off the plantation much so what was out there, we didn't know. I didn't know what she was describin', and when I looked up at everybody else, they just stared back, didn't say yes or no to if they heard her or not. They just stared and cried, 'cept Oseen. He hated Massah Duncan. He was in that same spot, lookin' the same way, nothin' changin'.

At that, Ms. Iney yanked the rope down that was around her neck so as to get free as she watched two men get shot down in their legs trying to run and rescue her while James stood there frozen in fear. The flames finally caught her, and the overseers dropped the rope to the dusty ground. Instead of running in every direction like a wild beast as the fire spread on her body, she took aim like she was already used to burning pains. She ran in the direction of freedom like she was running without any fire on her at all, until she fell down, setting the bushes on fire around her.

"Look at her! And that's what's gonna happen to every one of you who take to reading or trying to escape. Now you stand there and look at her. She ain't shoutin' no words of freedom now, is she? Go on and follow them gorilla directions if you like 'cause my hounds here like a good chase. You…little Wani," he called my name. "Wani!" he shouted, slamming his whip against the ground. Somebody shoved me forward, and I fell down, didn't know what to say. All I heard was Ms. Iney telling me to live. Just live. I was scared, so scared I was shakin' and crying at the same time. I looked back at Oseen and then James, then back at Oseen. I wanted him to help me, but he just stood there mad, not comin' for me at all.

Then, Massah Duncan came down to me and whispered in my ear. "Who else know how to read here? Now, you know won't nothin' happen to you. Tell me. Speak up!" he shouted.

My tears made his white face disappear when I looked up at him. I was so scared that my teeth shook in my mouth like it was a cold night outside. I saw my Ms. Iney over there burnin' to death, but that man didn't care nothin' about my tears. Then, when he pulled back the whip like he was gonna hit me with it, somethin' I ain't never had hit me before, I screamed out, "Nobody do. Nobody know how to read!" That was when I first learned how to deny my own self. It didn't matter how smart or fast or tall or strong I was. I knew that I had to lie about myself to myself and to white folks about myself or I was gonna die, just like Ms. Iney.

While I waited on that big, long whip to take all the skin off my body, he lowered it and walked away, back to the house and shut the door behind him. It was when Massah Duncan shut the door that Oseen rushed to come and get me. I was too scared, and from there, I had to look at Ms. Iney body burn all night long while her sister screamed behind me like she lost her own baby. That was the day I forgot how to talk. I used to talk all the time, but since learning how to lie on myself, I didn't want to. Was too scared to say somethin', anything, especially the truth. I couldn't speak. No words came out because they were just as scared of themselves as I was of them. It was that day that I started hating something more than anything I ever knew.

CHOOSE THE STORY'S FINAL PATH:

THE DAY I HATED FREEDOM – (Go to page 59)

THE DAY I TOOK FREEDOM – (Go to page 82)

THE DAY I HATED FREEDOM

"This the second day she ain't talkin'. Somethin' wrong with her. All she do is stare out yonder, eat and go to bed. We got to learn her to pick better, Oseen. Oseen?"

"I see that. Don't you know I see that, James? That there Ms. Iney," he whispered, "was the only family she… we know older than us here. She young still yet, and she ain't never seen nothin' like that before, not ever." He peeped over at her. "She gonna come outta that. She ain't got no choice, just like we ain't had no choice, 'cept when I was that age, I had some kin with me when it was my first time. Don't know how she feel. We all come up different. We make us kin. She got to learn to make more kin. We her kin. She need somebody, a lady, to latch on to like she did Ms. Iney. All she ever did was be with Ms. Iney."

"What you think gonna happen to her if she don't come outta her spell fast enough, huh? They gonna sell her or even worse, maybe even…"

77

"James, cut it now! She just need time. We doin' good with the crops and cotton we get. She not yet in her right age to pick how the older ones do, and they know that. She gone be fine. They don't even know she like how she is yet, so don't go bringin' attention to it. Just you and all the others say nothing, but if you have to, say she sick in the stomach."

"For how long, Oseen? A sick stomach forever? Massah gone kill that girl! He gone sell her, maybe even kill her if she don't come on to her mind! That's 'xactly what they do to us if we don't act like what is normal."

"Well it won't be her fault, now will it?" he shouted. "Just like it ain't Ms. Iney fault she where she is!"

James's head fell low, and he stumbled away from Oseen. "I'm goin' out now to the fields 'for..."

"Look here, James. I ain't mean that like it came, so angry, but I am mad...mad about the whole thing and Lil Wani. I ain't blamin' you, son."

"I ain't your son!" he cried as the tears fell down his face. "I ain't got no papa and mama dead,

78

and I know what I did. I wrote it! I know you know it was me! I buried it, Oseen. Don't know how it came up to show from that dirt, but I know how to bury," he continued feeling hopeless. "It came up somehow, and I can't fix it. I shoulda died, not Ms. Iney," he cried.

"No no. Don't you go doin' that, James. Come on," he said, reaching his strong arms around him to hug some of the pain out of him. As James felt like he couldn't go on, Oseen looked back, he looked right back at me. I saw him, just like I heard their whole conversation, but I didn't talk. I couldn't talk. It wasn't James fault nothin'. It was mine. I was too scared. If everybody found out, everybody was gonna tell on me. They was gonna hate me and kill me theyself because I let Massah see us with Freedom. I made Ms. Iney die. I hated Freedom, and it hated me. I didn't wanna talk. I just listened to them. I was gonna die if I talked. Just like Oseen told me, and he was right. I should've kept my mouth shut sometimes, most times.

"Listen here, James. I'm not your papa or your mama, but I needs you just like you needs me. Don't go out there showin' nothing on your inside. Keep your heart and your head to yourself. This ain't your fault. Ms. Iney would tell us that…this life ain't our fault, and you knowing how to do something good like reading ain't no shame just like wantin' freedom ain't no shame. She was glad to die for ya. I know that for a real thing 'cause you got a better chance to get what she didn't have. Now stand up here. I'm your papa 'til you find another one or 'til you get grown enough 'til you don't need one. Stand up. Just like Ms. Iney tried, I'mma try to get y'all some freedom, and that there gonna be my freedom, gettin' freedom for y'all. Watch and see."

James let go of him, and Oseen spoke again. "Sorry for what I said. We in this together, and when we split up one day as they do us, we still in this together, no matter where we are. It hurt, but soon it won't. You got tears, but I got to find my tears. Ain't seen 'em in a while now. They don't help nothin'. Be strong. Keep thinkin' and learnin' 'til you can do it in the open. Keep it where it can't be seen, James, all the time." He saw the tremblin' in James's body. "Stop showin' your fear…and don't keep guilt. White man say you guilty for stuff that ain't a crime. You ain't do nothin' wrong by writin'. They just don't want you to 'cause they wanna control how smart and able we get. Next time you wanna write, write it underneath your eyelids and in your head and your chest."

After the talk, James headed out to the fields, and then Oseen turned to me. My eyes was cracked when he walked on over, and I saw how he was lookin', like he didn't want nobody to walk in and see him come up to me. He knew I was awake, but the closer he got, the scareder I got. I ain't want nobody to say nothin' to me.

"Stop that shakin', Lil Wani. You shakin' like it's cold out. You can't keep on doin' this. We need you to open up your mouth like you used to," he continued, panting like he was out of breath but didn't run anywhere, "so we can know you alright." He looked behind him really fast, and turned back around just as quick as he did that. Then, he reached over to

81

my big toe like he was tryin' to play with me, and I pulled it back because I didn't know what he was gonna do. He ain't never hurt me before, but it felt like if anybody came near me, it was gonna hurt. Seem like other people who even talked about what I heard him and James talkin' about – Freedom – was gonna get me hurt or they was gonna get hurt.

Tears rolled down my face, and even that hurt me. Every time I looked away from his face, I saw them flames. That hot fire…it came closer the closer he came, and Massah's voice right there in my head like he lived inside there. I shook my head back and forth tryin', closin' my eyeballs tight, to shake him out of my head, and then I felt his hand on my ankle. I couldn't even breathe no more.

"Lil Wani?"

I knew that was Oseen's voice, but it wasn't nowhere near louder than Massah's. That fire kept comin' 'round me like I was sittin' in a pot of stew outdoors, and it was makin' me hot and I felt like I was burnin' like Ms. Iney, like he was draggin', me by my ankle to throw me over in the fire, too. Ms.

Iney's sister was screamin' right along with Massah's warnings in my ears, yellin' at me so loud like she been doin' every night since Ms. Iney gave her life. Her sister was always comin' to me at night, screamin' at me, and her face looked to be Ms. Iney on one side while her own face was on the other side. She was a monster, tellin' me she saw me with that paper when I buried it and that she gonna tell that it was me who wrote it. She kept screamin' "*I'mma tell! I'mma tell it. I'mma tell it all!*".

I pushed my hands against my ears to make her screamin' stop, but it wouldn't. She kept screamin' and screamin', and then I felt her touch me on my shoulder. Where did Oseen go?

"Oseen!" I screamed. The wood at the corner of the cabin wouldn't break no matter how hard I beat it and knocked my whole body against it. Then, my body came up off the ground. She was pickin' me up! I screamed but ain't know who to scream for because I didn't have nobody. I was by myself. Wasn't nothing but fire comin' down on my head, and when I looked down, there wasn't nothin' but fire down there, too, with Ms. Iney runnin' through the flames. I was 'bout to burn, too.

"Stop screamin'. Stop screamin'!"

Another hand touched me, but it was over my mouth, and all the other hands that was on me let go. The fire disappeared when a hand went over my mouth. I fought so hard, hittin' at a face I didn't know until I got tired of fightin'. Then the hand came off my mouth, and I looked up. It was Oseen again.

"They gone put me in the fire with Ms. Iney," I cried, tryin' to crawl up his body as I felt his arms cradle me like I was a new baby.

"Lil Wani…Lil Wani…I'm right here. This Oseen, and ain't nobody puttin' you in no fire. What you talkin' 'bout now? I knew you would start talkin' again," he said with a little smile that went away fast as he sat me down on the only chair in the cabin. "It's time to go out in them fields now, 'fore Massah Duncan say somethin' 'bout why we ain't showin' you and …"

"Take it out of me," I cried. "I don't want it no more. It hurt everybody, and I don't want it."

"What you sayin', Lil Wani? Take what out of you? Come on now, and put some of this water here on your face, swallow some, and let's gone on out there so least somebody can see you, that you walkin', talkin' and breathin'. You got to gone out there..."

He tugged on my arm, but I ain't move. I wasn't gonna move 'til Freedom came out of me. "Ms. Iney, she burned up and it was 'cause of Freedom. I don't wanna read. I don't wanna know how, and I don't wanna write ever. Freedom ain't no good for me, not for you or me, and you need to get it outta you, too, or we gonna die!"

"Shut your mouth up now," he whispered. "Shut it up. These walls ain't nothin' but wood from trees. They got lil holes in it so the overseers can hear us. Thin wood so they can hear us. Shhh," he said, putting me down to walk over to the door and listen, then to the wall. "Listen here, you stay put. Hold your stomach tight if they come lookin' for you. They will think you been sick."

"They gonna kill me?"

"No, no…"

"They will. They know 'bout what I did. She told me. Ms. Iney sister. She come to tell me at night," I rushed and told. "She say she gonna tell on me, and they gonna get me, and I ain't got no place to run and hide."

"'Bout what you did?" He hopped beside me like somebody stuck him with a pin, got down on his knees and shook my arms. "'Bout what you did? Is that why you scared? What you done done, Lil Wani?" He ran back to the door of the cabin, made sure nobody was coming, and then fell back in front of me. "You got to hurry up. I'm supposed to be out there in them fields. They gonna be lookin' for me as I'm the strongest hand."

"I didn't cover it back up good, the words on that paper Massah 'dem found. I had it that day, and I thought I put it back, but I didn't. Don't nobody know that but me, but seem like Ms. Iney sister know 'cause she come to me in my dreams and…"

"She ever come in real life?" When I didn't answer him, he asked again. "Come on, Lil Wani, did she?"

"No."

He fell backwards onto the floor of the cabin, rubbed his hand down his sweaty face and then took a deep breath. "It was you who got that paper from the ground, and you didn't cover it back up right?"

I shook my head up and down.

"Look here. Don't you tell nobody what you done told me, you hear me? Nobody. If somebody even know you had some paper in your hand, they gonna test you. It's me and Ms. Iney know you can read, but nobody else right?"

I nodded.

"Alright. Alright. There's a reason why you're dreamin' that. I'mma go out here in the fields. I'mma be back. You stay put. You sick...ain't nothin' wrong with you, but you just sick...sick in the stomach. And don't be talkin' nowhere near Ms. Iney sister."

He ran out the cabin and left me in there scared of what was gonna happen to me next. I sat there so scared that the wood started breakin' apart, and the smoke started comin' in. I held my breath because I knew if I walked out that door, Freedom was comin' to destroy me. Ms. Iney's ashes was right out there to remind me.

I stayed inside, in one spot, 'til all the tobacco and cotton was done for the day. One lady came in to give me food during the day. She would put it by the door or bring it right to me. Another one would walk by and pretend like she was only walkin' but would peep in to check on me. I saw all the ladies that day but one. I didn't see Ms. Iney's sister. By the time the sun set off the fields, I was asleep again, but instead of Ms. Iney sister comin' in my dream, somethin' shook me awake.

"Shhh...we got to go. Don't talk. I'm 'bout to pick you up, and we runnin'. Somebody saw you."

I hung onto Oseen like he was my only life. My neck and face fit right onto his big neck, and he didn't even have to hold me none as he ran because I was holdin' just that tight. My lil head was bangin' hard against his shoulder, and I kept lookin' back to see if anybody was behind us. Wasn't nobody, but he still didn't tell who saw me. After he stopped to take a break, he put me down so we could drink some water from a spring. Then, I asked him.

"Who saw me?"

He stopped drinkin' and sat down on the ground, looking at it like he never seen it before. "Ain't nobody really saw you. I just didn't want you to ask no questions that I ain't had time to answer. Reason we had to run though is 'cause of the story of somebody seein' somethin' they ain't really seen. That somebody was James. James was talkin' to Ms. Iney sister, and I heard him talkin' 'bout our secret, that we can read, and that I was the real one who wrote the note. Say he know 'cause he saw me do it. She started cryin' and after she stopped cryin', she had a look on her face that could kill ten hogs and five white men all at once. That there was when I knew, I needed to run. We need to run. James just don't know that he done got all us killed. White man ain't got no discretion. Them dreams you had was a warnin' from God, and I took it as it was me 'posed

89

to get you out of there since James let our secret go. Your grandpapa, he used to dream them dreams, too, and 'fore they took his tongue from him, he would tell us."

"But you ain't write that stuff down. James was lyin' on you 'cause it was James who did it. I just found it. I knew it was James back before they killed Ms. Iney. I heard 'em talkin'. That's when I found out I didn't cover it up good."

"You knew?"

"Yeah, 'cause when Ms. Iney give herself up, she did it for him first, then for us. She gave up her life for us because she was tired of livin'. She said when you get tired of livin', we supposed to tell we can read."

"Ms. Iney say that?"

"She said that. You don't remember?"

"Maybe she mean it like this," he said, standin' up from the spring to look around. "Maybe she mean to say to keep your mouth closed so you won't die. I don't believe she was tired of livin'. I believe she was tired of seein' other folk she love die, so she prefer to die for 'em so she don't have to feel it no more." He walked over to me. "Listen here. I'm gonna take you somewhere. Take you to somebody I know. Somebody you should know already but ain't nobody knew 'bout him but me and Ms. Iney." He looked around again. "I'mma take you to be with your papa before you go with me so you will always know what he look like and what his name be. It done came to this, and I made a promise. I can't take you with me 'lesson he know I am. Make me feel like one of them whites, like how they take us away from our families. Your papa, he done stayed close."

My mind didn't know what he was sayin'. I ain't never had a papa, and I ain't never, ever had a mama, so how was it that I can have a papa with no mama? Oseen was more my papa than anybody I ever knew.

"I ain't got a papa." I was mad. I didn't know what I was mad at, but I was mad. "I ain't going with no other body. You can't make me!"

"Yes you will. He woulda' died if anybody woulda' said somethin', even your mama, so we left it. We was the only ones, plus her papa, who she could trust. We left it like we didn't know, even after you grow up like you do. Wasn't no danger that way, for him or you, and you'll learn that where there ain't no danger, keep it that way. It's danger now. What's gonna happen if they get me and you together? What's gonna happen when James himself gotta get rid of you somehow 'cause of what you know? How you know that he can read? If he scared now, what you think could happen to you?"

I didn't answer. I didn't answer 'cause I couldn't. I didn't answer 'cause I knew. We would get the fire. We would get the fire just like Ms. Iney.

"Here's what's gonna happen. They gonna kill me, and if James don't get you before Massah do, then they gonna beat you 'til you say somethin'. When you say somethin', you gonna tell on James, and then he gonna die, too. Later, Ms. Iney sister gonna have a bad feelin' 'bout you 'til you come up dead yourself. Ain't nothin' good coming out of this. James shoulda' been the one died. Ms. Iney, she loved him and tried her best, but he's scary, so scary I could smell it on him. He was too young, just like you are, too young to hold yourself. Too young. You break. That's why I had to take you with me. I don't want you to break like him."

"Here is something else you need to know. There ain't nothing good 'bout a lady like Amy, Iney sister, when she get mad and sad at the same time. Now come on. Massah Duncan is bad, but he ain't worse than Amy would be to you. Ain't nothin' worse than your own kind killin' you or not givin' you peace when the whites sleep. You won't make it to next year. You already dreamin'. Least you got a chance, a slim one, comin' with me. It's a big circle like that, Lil Wani. Hand of one Negro in trouble, hand of all of us, one way or another, they gonna get us all, and we end up turnin' on each other. You always got to know when to escape the circle if you can. Whatever you do, if things go wrong, don't you be 'lone with that Amy…not ever. Just stay alive, Lil Wani. Stay alive. Get your freedom."

"I don't want Freedom! Freedom gonna kill me!" I screamed. I shouted so loud that my own throat hurt, and Oseen shut it. He shut it quick. His hand went around my mouth, and then he picked me up and ran even harder. I didn't know where we were going because I never been off the plantation. I never even seen Oseen leave the plantation, but he acted like he knew where he was runnin', like he really did know where I had a papa. Then, after he got a ways down and I was quiet, he stopped and turned back around just to pace around a tree. I heard him start cryin' for the first time, and then he put me down.

"Lil Wani, in order for you to have more protection, I need you to jump 'cross this here place, from here to there, and then I need you to jump back across here to me. Hurry up now so we can keep movin'." He wiped the tears from his eyes, and before I could even ask him why I needed to jump back and forth across the land, he stopped me from talking. "Lil Wani, just do it. Jump over there and then jump back here so we can go."

That was what I done. There wasn't nothing but flat grass underneath this big ole tree. I didn't see nothing to jump over, so I just jumped from one side of the tree to the other side. I did it quick, too, because I never saw him cry before, not even when Ms. Iney died. I jumped over there and then jumped back over to him. When I was done, he stared at the ground, looked at me and then picked me back up to keep runnin'. I turned back to look at the place underneath that tree where I jumped back and forth. I kept lookin' until all the other trees moved in the way of my sight. Somethin' made Oseen cry, and it was somethin' back there at that tree. I didn't wanna ask him because it seemed like it was makin' it harder for him to move faster.

It took us some more movin' before we got to another open field. That was when he put me down and told me to walk behind him. His fists was raised up, and I got even more scared than I already was. Then, he grabbed my hand and took off runnin' with me to an old cabin that I could barely see in the dark. We wasn't hidden by the trees no more. I was in plain sight but with no sight because it was pitch black, and I was scared to death.

When we got to the cabin, Oseen didn't open the cabin door, but instead, he walked around the side and poked a long stick through a hole in the wood. The cabin was bigger than the ones we all shared back on Massah's plantation. I watched Oseen keep movin' around the stick until it was pulled from his hands, and I didn't see it no more. Then, there was a tap back on the wall of the cabin. After that, somebody opened the door and came out.

I scooted behind Oseen. I held on to his pants so tight that when he reached back to get me with his arms, it took him more than two tugs to get me off his pants and high up in the air in front of his face.

He was talkin' to me, but I didn't hear him. I just kept grabbin' at his neck and then his hair. Every time he moved my hand from his body, the other one would squeeze a piece of him tight. I was scared to shout again because I knew there was a Massah somewhere 'round, and I was gonna get caught. I didn't wanna be where I was. I wanted to be back there where we ran from, back in the past, when it was just fine. When I had Ms. Iney and never knew nothin' 'bout freedom. I was safe, even without a mama and papa, I was safe.

Suddenly, I felt two more hands wrap around my waist, and I couldn't hold on to Oseen no more. I started to cry out, but Oseen seemed like he didn't care none. He just stared at me in the dark. He didn't even move to get me back. He just stood there and watched me cry 'til I was turned around by a new man, a man that I never saw ever in my whole life.

"Wani."

He didn't call me Lil Wani. He called me Wani. He had a deep voice, way deeper than Oseen's. He was darker than Oseen was, too, and taller, and as he put me down to the ground, he came down with me and started talkin' again.

"Wani. Stop cryin'. You ain't got to cry no more. I'm not here to hurt you. I been checkin' on you all your life. You been growin' good. My name is Ayao. I'm your papa. Before you even say somethin', I couldn't say nothin'. I couldn't. It was your mama and me that coulda' caused a fury over there because your mama...wasn't nobody supposed to love her," he stumbled, "but I ended up lovin' her in secret, it had to be in secret, 'less they woulda killed me."

"Only reason you alive now Lil Wani, is 'cause they ain't know for sure who …" Oseen started, but stopped when my papa Ayao started talkin' again.

"They ain't know that you look like my own mama. That be where you come from. They thought you mighta' come from somebody else on that plantation. That woulda' been good to them, but you didn't. They didn't know for sure. But I know for sure. I see her picture, my mama's picture, in your face. That's how you can know you mine. You my daughter. She was what they call mulatto. My papa, she told me, was a dark man like me, and look here at the side of your neck. That be where my mama birth mark was, too. Same shape and all, just like my sister's own. Lil Wani, you my baby. You look just like her, 'cept just a little browner is all, and you look just like your mama, too. You got the mark that runs in my family with the women. I had to keep you being my child a secret 'less we both die, me and your mama. I couldn't never meet you, but I always kept up with you, through Oseen, Ms. Iney..."

"Ms. Iney gone, Ayao. I had to bring her. It's dangerous times now, for me and her."

"What happened to her?"

"They lynch her. Lynch her for readin', writin', just days ago … but it wasn't her. Person who did it, still there and done told a story 'bout it was me to her sister. Won't be long for the word get back to Massah Duncan and he find out the truth one by one. I wasn't stayin', and I wasn't gonna let her stay… not when she got you. She at the age where he could hurt her." He paused. "She can read, Ayao. She gonna have the truth squeezed out her, and you know it. We all in trouble."

"Now I'm 'bout to die." I looked back at Oseen and then back at my new papa. "That's why I got to go with you, so I won't die. I got to go with you so Freedom won't get me."

"What you mean?" He looked up at Oseen confused and then back down at me. "What you talkin' 'bout, *so Freedom won't get you*? Freedom is

99

what you want, Wani." He rubbed my hand in his big hand, but I pulled it back.

"No it ain't. It was Freedom that got Ms. Iney burned up in that fire." I leaned over to whisper in his ear. "She was readin', and she was writin' just like another person. I'm gonna forget mine, though, how to read, so I won't get the fire. Freedom ain't good for us, papa." I took his hand back and tried to pull him back in the cabin, but he didn't come. "You say you my papa, ain't it?" I looked at Oseen. "Come on, Oseen. We safe now." Oseen stood there like he had somethin' else to do, like he wasn't gonna stay.

"I am your papa, but I can't come in witcha. Not right now. Wani, in order that you don't die, me and Oseen..." he paused, "Or either me by myself...have to go and stop them from takin' or killin' you. They comin', and we already had a plan in case they find you, just in case some danger come to the plantation. If I don't come back..."

"You comin' back," Oseen interrupted. "We got another way. I thought of one, and it includes me. We got to get goin' now though. Right now before day breaks. That way, we can be back to get Lil Wani, and keep on goin'."

"Wani, go inside with her. That be Sally. If I don't come back here, you stay put, right inside this cabin here where Sally tell you. Don't come out none."

I looked over at a figure standin' at the side of the cabin. It was a lady, and she held her hand out for me. Before I went over to her, my papa grabbed me and kissed me on my cheek. It was the first kiss I ever got from my real papa.

"What if you don't never come back? Do I stay here forever?"

"If I don't never come back, there be one thing that will keep you alive and Sally will tell you how to do that. You will keep it like it's the truth. You won't know it 'til she tell it. Wani…Freedom is your best friend." He looked up at the lady and then back at me. "I'm a free man." I snatched my hand from him as soon as he said it. He reached back over to me, but I moved back from him still until Oseen stopped me. Then, Ayao reached out and touched my hand again. I let him take it.

"These white folk don't want you to have it, so it's not Freedom that hurt us. It's them. I bought mine, and I bought Sally's. Workin' on buyin' yours, but ain't know if I could because word was that Massah Duncan wasn't gonna ever let you go. Besides that, they want it all to themselves that freedom, the nice house, the warm shoes, the blankets in the winter, and the food at the table and the smiles on the faces of their families..."

"And the readin' and writin'?"

"That, too. Ain't no sense in hatin' Freedom. It make you feel good. It made Ms. Iney feel good, good enough that she gave her own life for it. Remember what I say to you. Freedom is what you want. That's what I'm going to get for you, even if you don't see me no mo'. I love you, and you gonna have freedom."

He held me there, huggin' me and lookin' at me for some time 'fore Oseen came and pat me on the top of my head, stroked my cheek and smiled. Sally brought him something wrapped up in a cloth and handed him some papers, then they both ran off. When I got inside with that woman named Sally, she started in, tellin' me all my family names, over and over again. She didn't stop, and I couldn't shut my eyes to sleep. I couldn't remember 'em, but she also told me that if I couldn't remember who the name was assigned to, that I was supposed to name my children the names I remembered when I got to be a woman. The names was supposed to keep track somehow, like mine and my mama's. She said the older people around me would be able to tell me my story then. She was right, too. Ms. Iney told me about myself because my name was Wani, and she remembered my mama. I just didn't know if the man that I called my papa was gonna make it back to me.

By sunrise, he wasn't back yet, so I stayed put, just like he told me to do. I kept sayin' all those names of people I never met over and over again in my head so my voice wouldn't carry out of the cabin by sayin' them out loud. I was scared. Yes, I was scared. More than my own papa, I wanted Oseen back because I knew him more. I knew how when he got mad, he wasn't gonna hurt me. I knew when he was supposed to be sleep, he wasn't half the time. I knew he always mean what he say. I didn't know my papa like that. He seemed like he was nice though. He said he loved me. Oseen didn't say that. He didn't have to. I just knew he did.

Even though I knew my papa said he loved me, and I knew Oseen didn't have to say he loved me, neither one of 'em came back for me. I waited for two days, and on the night of that second day, Sally came inside the cabin cryin', holdin' her stomach and throwin up food all over the place. I took a rag to try and wipe it up, but she pushed me away from her. When I tried again to go to the door of the cabin to get some water out the bucket, she yanked me back…but it was too late. I figured out why she wanted me back. It wasn't just 'cause I wasn't supposed to be there. It was 'cause I saw the body of my new papa bein' carried by three men into that open field me and Oseen ran through to get him. I didn't know what to feel, but I 'membered what he told me to do.

I ran back in my corner. He didn't listen to me. I knew I was right. Freedom did it. I knew Freedom killed Oseen, too. Later, I ended up with Sally. She called me free, but I didn't feel free. That was the end of my papa and Oseen. I still hated Freedom even though Sally told me each day after me seein' my real papa dead that I had it and had to keep it for a long time.

She told me the story of what was told to her, that my papa and Oseen went with my papa's money to buy me from Massah Duncan. Before the sun came up though, Massah Duncan had already got word of what James lied about. He got it from Ms. Iney sister. When Oseen and papa got to the plantation, some of the others saw him and held him back, saying that the overseers was already out searchin' for him and me. Told him to hide, but Oseen didn't hide. Papa didn't neither. Oseen saw movement from in Massah Duncan's house. He knew the overseers were gone but Massah Duncan was still there. They told Sally that was when Oseen and my papa split up.

Everybody on the plantation let Oseen just run up and take the life of James and Ms. Iney sister. Said they both caused more harm to the whole flock than good, so they had to go. Said Oseen, though he loved James, hit him one good time and that boy was gone. They said Oseen didn't even look like himself after that. Said he was moanin' so much they thought he was gonna die himself. Then, he went to get Ms. Iney sister, but when he got to her, she had already took her own life out behind her cabin. Said a knife had done cut from one side to the other of her own neck. Then, they shoved him to run on. If he didn't run, he was gonna be a lynched man sooner than later. That was what he did. He left my papa.

Nobody knew what happened to papa. Nobody was there. When papa met with Massah Duncan at the house, he took Massah Duncan by shock. Say my papa went inside that house, but there was a shot after say five minutes. Next thing, papa was drug out the house, and Massah was shoutin' and yellin' for me. Said he was hollerin' Wani real loud, but when I didn't come, they covered for me, said that Oseen took me, ran off with me and killed the others. They pointed in the opposite direction than what Oseen really ran.

All I know was that they never found me. My name was Wani, and I was free with a woman I call mama named Sally. That was who the papers say she was to me. They had fake papers for me already made up, but I had to keep rememberin' my real name Wani because on the papers I had to say something different. On them papers, my name was Nami. I also had a last name. It was my papa's last name – Newman. Said he gave himself that name, and that was who I was supposed to be so long as I was free.

After all that, I still hated Freedom even more. It took everything from me. Everything and everybody. I couldn't hear Ms. Iney talk to me, I couldn't have Oseen make me feel protected, and I couldn't have but that short time with my papa Ayao. If they didn't want Freedom so much, I woulda' still had 'em, wouldn't I?

I ain't never got over my hatred for Freedom even though I ended up glad to be free. If somebody asked me would I trade it to see my own family again, see my real papa and meet my mama, and even see the man who sing so much that they took his tongue for fightin'...my grandpa...or even see Ms. Iney and Oseen, just to laugh and live with 'em 'stead of makin' another way from the time I was little, my answer might shock a whole heap of people. A whole heap. I can't help how I feel, even down in this here grave. My slavery ain't end though I was free. I was chained up, hurt up and confused on the inside. Ain't never figured out how to get free from the inside like I was on the outside. Never. That's why I still hate Freedom because it been hurtin' me all my life from the inside 'cause of what it took from me. Folks would say I saw it backwards, but they just didn't wanna see it how it was for me.

THE END

(Go back to page 97 to choose the story's other final path)

THE DAY I TOOK FREEDOM

I ain't never got madder than what I got that day, the day I stood back there watchin' Ms. Iney die. My teeth clinched back my words, and my fists beat into my own legs so hard that I thought they was gonna break. I ain't got too many words to describe how I felt, but I know I wanted to kill. I never have had too many words no how, but I had a rage that lasted so long 'til it made me ache to kill what kept givin' it to me. So don't look for no explanation 'cept for this one. It was a rage that finally let loose. It finally let loose, and I watched it take... take our Freedom since nobody was givin' it to us.

There wasn't a chirp from the trees, but the breeze was whistlin' to me, whisperin' to me. I heard it like it had teeth and a tongue and could talk. It knew my language, and it talked to me like when I was a little boy. Most folk couldn't hear the breeze like I could, and I knew that 'cause if they did, they wouldn't be sleepin' through the talk. They would be listenin'.

I looked around at their stomachs goin' up and down and they backs risin' and fallin' as I tipped on by 'em. Couldn't barely see nothin', but I knowed where they laid and how they laid. Ole John couldn't sleep on his side 'cause that hit he took from that white man a whiles back caused him pain ever since. He slept on his back. Caper, he slept on his stomach 'cause his back stayed peelin'. He ain't never healed right from the whip. Some days it looked fine and some days it leak out, and we had to patch it up. A fever set in, and he would be so hot 'til he was cold. He would get in trouble for bein' sick, a sick he didn't ask for, but a sick that was put on him by the whip.

As I stepped outside, the wind stopped talkin'. I'd done harbored a long knife in my shack for a long time, and as I looked over there where Ms. Iney burned up 'fore my very eyes, I promised myself that I wasn't gonna let my knife go…not for no whip nor for no white man. Guns…they only shoot what they see. Massah wasn't gonna see me. Nobody was. I was gonna need just my knife, my heart, and my hands. Knives and hands kill what they can touch. Hearts kill everything beforehand.

I never slept good since I came as a grown man on these fields that I work that ain't even mine. It ain't fittin' to sleep on a land that you don't own. Ms. Iney used to tell me, she say... "Oseen, one day, you watch. One day." She always had this hope in her from somewhere, like she knew somethin' I didn't, like she saw somethin' God showed her or lived somethin' that I didn't know nothin' 'bout, but she didn't show me. I figured she was talkin' 'bout gettin' freedom one day. Far as my eyes could see, which was clear past the fields, just a piece of freedom for a day would be worth runnin' for. Get to laugh without a whip snatchin' it, and get to moan for somethin' 'cept death, pain, hunger and loss. Get to moan for happiness sometimes instead. Even when a baby was born, because of them chains, I hated it was born. I loved the little children, just like Lil Wani, but I done seen what they did to 'em, did to her – made her scared to find what she ain't never seen on people like us. I wasn't scared to find it, and I wasn't scared to get it either. Not no more. I was gonna get my Freedom.

As I walked to Massah house, even the dogs didn't know what's going on. I was just that quiet. When a man walked the same ground for so long, doing the same things from sun up to sun down, he learned the heartbeat of the ground. He knew when it's gonna thump and when it was gonna be silent. I knew when to walk left of the beat and walk right of the beat with my eyes closed tight. My feet knew how to land on the ground to not make a sound.

Massah always had that overseer sittin' on the porch all night, watchin' us like he wasn't one of us. I used to watch him every single night. I did. I would imagine myself skinnin' him alive and showin' him what he looked like, what his skin looked like, just so he could figure out how he shouldn't watch against us for the white man. He fell asleep on that porch when the night got deep, and as I made my way up the porch, he didn't hear me comin'. The wind blew hard, and I stopped. My toes was right there on the edge of that step, and that old colored overseer's chest took in a deep breath as I paused only one foot away from him. His eyes didn't come open, but before his chest raised again, I was on him. I made sure he wouldn't enjoy anymore deep breaths like that last one that I saw him take ever again. The more I remembered Ms. Iney, the more I squeezed 'til I took his life. Before he fell and made a loud noise, I cradled his head and led it to the porch. Then, I took his gun, not because I needed it, but because somebody else mighta' got it and used it on me.

He was better off dead. Massah told him to hit me with a whip, and he did it instead of takin' that whip and hittin' Massah with it. He was wastin' his life sittin' on the porch to sleep in the summer and the spring, instead of a cabin, watchin' over a man who call him slave. I wished I coulda' woke him back up from the dead and shoved his head in the waters so he could see his reflection as he died, but that was all I could do with him, so I let him lay there dead before I carried on.

I didn't want to use the door to get inside because it creaked all the time, so I tried that window that always stayed up in the daytime. I figured it either would move or it wouldn't, but if it did, it would be quiet. When I pushed on it just a little bit, it moved up. The latch was broke. I knew that 'cause each and every day, I saw how they just pulled back the curtains and lifted it up. Wasn't no move to the latch. At the end of the day, they would push it down with no move to the latch at that time neither. I climbed in.

It wasn't quiet in there. Seem like the scream of death on the porch and the peace of the wind outdoors was nothin' to the noise in the big house. I nearly jumped back out the window, but I had to stay there and listen to all the noise that scared me until I didn't hear it no more. Sweat poured down my neck and arms like I just stood up from inside a high river. My mouth went dry. Then, after I stood there for a while, I ain't hear nothin' else. All that noise of screamin' and death was in my own head. I checked back outside through the window that I entered through. Nobody saw me.

I knew where he slept at night, so that was where I started steppin' to. When I got there, I peeked inside. There was people in the bed, sound asleep. I heard the breathing, so I walked on inside the dark room. The closer I got, I turned the gun around in my hand to not touch the trigger because I didn't want to shoot. I wanted to bang the life out of him just like he banged the life out of us. I didn't want the knife to take his life too fast, so I tucked it back in my pants. It was only when I got up closer that I seen Massah Duncan wasn't in the bed.

I spun around like I'd done seen the dead, and the noise started again. First, it started back with the sound of the breathin' coming from the bed. It was so loud that I couldn't hear my own self think. I got my knife back in my hand and pointed it at everything that made a sound. Noise was my enemy just as much as Massah was, and anything that moved too close, I was gonna skin alive.

My feet wouldn't move easy anymore, so I dragged them to a wall and stood there, being as quiet as I could be. The sweat on my body already reached the floor, and out the corner of my eye, I saw Massah's wife shuffle. The noise grew louder in the house, like white men from everywhere was shoutin' for my own death, and as they kept shoutin' and I kept hearin' the whip hit the floor at my feet, I jumped from my corner. Full of rage at the thought of her screamin' for my kill like she done to others times before, I leaped on her back and hands to pin them behind her. It ain't take long for me to take her life, and after that, all the whips that came in for me like snakes slithered on out the room as she stopped fightin'. Her face was still in the pillow. She was still.

I nearly fell back onto the floor but caught myself. When my foot touched the floor again, the noises started back up. Where was Massah Duncan? That was when I lifted the gun, what I thought I wouldn't have to use, and by then, the whole floor was covered in salt water, and I felt like I was gonna drown in my own sweat. I got dizzy, so I swam out of the room and fell against the side of the door. I could breathe again, but I'd made a sound. It was my first sound. I knew I made it 'cause the shoutin' stopped around me, but then I smelled flesh burnin'.

Runnin' to look, I stumbled across the floor past a room so I could get to that hallway window that looked out at the slave quarters, but when I pulled back the curtain, wasn't no fire on no flesh. It wasn't no fire at all, not even smoke. Then I heard it. I heard him. I turned around, and there he was standin' over me like a tower, but he was really shorter than I ever been. Still yet, he was over me, and he was laughin' at me. He stood there like the devil himself and had a big ole smile like he was about to put a lashin' to me or worse. I blinked my eyes and held up that gun, and when I did, everything changed. He wasn't standin' over me and laughin' no more. Instead, he was tremblin' and had already started runnin', stumblin' away from me. He was naked down to his underwear, and instead of shootin', I ran after him, tackled him down, and started whippin' him like he whipped me all them times. I needed to know how it felt to beat him to death. I needed to know if I liked beatin' him as much as he liked beatin' me. Every time I hit him, I heard screams in my ears of everybody he done killed in front of me. Them there screams helped me to keep hittin' him 'til I'd done mangled his face. I hit him so much 'til his eye was hanging loose out the socket, and I saw the pain of my own self in his body. I couldn't recognize my own pain it was so bad, so I didn't wanna recognize him or what he looked like no more. Then, I stopped. I stopped it right there, sat back and laughed. I ain't had no massah no more. They ain't had no massah no more. We ain't had no massah no more.

I soon killed the other two overseers on the land where they rested, and I stole they guns. I kept spinnin' 'round and 'round in the night with the blood of evil men coverin' my hands. My bloody hands wasn't from no murders. I wasn't no bad man, and I wasn't no evil one like them neither. My hands was the bloody hands of the freedom that I took, that I had to take, that was rightfully my own and my people own! I was proud, and for the first time in my life, I felt like my *own* man, like I owned myself. Wasn't a sad bone in my body, and it made me so happy that I woke everybody up 'round me so they could see, see the good thing I done for all of us.

They was afraid at first when they saw me. I had to prove to 'em that it was all over and that we was free. I showed 'em the guns, and I ran back inside the big house and got food – ate it right in front of 'em.

"We free. We free. James…y'all, look here," I said, snatching another bun and eatin' it. "Ain't we cook it? It's ours now, from our own hands." The blood was still on my hands, all dried up, and when James and the rest saw how I was eatin' and nobody was comin' to hang me high, they all ran in the house, and I watched.

None of us ever slept in a comfortable bed like them or sat in the seats they sat in before. Even the Negroes who worked in the house wasn't allowed to sit in them seats. They stood up all day long. We was gonna sit in 'em that night. Of all the people was dancin' and shoutin' and rushin' to get ready to run so nobody catch us all. I saw everybody celebratin', but one I didn't see. It was Lil Wani. She stood there at the door of the cabin scared to move her little body out the shack. That there was when I walked over to her, took her by her wrist and yanked her mind free.

"I took it, Lil Wani. I got us Freedom. It feel good," I said kneelin' down to see her face to face. "This here…this here is what Ms. Iney wanted you to have. She wanted me to have it, so I had to get it for us. You remember, 'member always that Freedom, Freedom for us, it got to be taken, so you take it." She saw that smile come across my face, and she stopped shiverin' in the hot night. I could tell right then that she didn't feel that whip waitin' for her backside no more. For the first time, I watched a lil Negro child feel free, and it felt good to me. Made me even gladder that I killed Massah and 'nem.

"It feel real good, Lil Wani. It don't make you go quiet. Ain't no need for you to be scared. You the last baby girl that's gonna be scared with me around.

You hear that noise? It make you smile. Come on. Go inside."

Inside there was dancin' and singin' and shoutin', and nobody cared about the blood, the bodies on the porch or in the house. For the first time, there were real smiles, real joy, and as I watched Lil Wani take her first steps of freedom, she looked back at where Ms. Iney was burned to death, waved, then she looked up at me.

"Ain't nobody gonna kill me?"

"No. I did what your grandpapa tried to do for you. You free now. Ain't nobody gonna kill you. Stop being scared. That was the last day you gonna be scared just to live."

Then, she ran over to everyone else and started playin' like she ain't never played before. The night was like broad daylight. I looked back over at Ms. Iney.

"I took care of her. I took care of all of 'em. Just me. Oseen."

When I got back in the house, I went plunderin' and found some money and papers. I could read, so I did just that after puttin' money in my pockets that we was gonna need to pay our way with the fake papers I was gonna fix up in my writin'. When I sorted the papers, I found what looked like an important letter and read it, but as the words came 'cross my eyes, I fell backwards onto the floor, squeezin' the paper tight and starin' at it like it was sayin' somethin' that I was readin' wrong. The words on the letter said we was already free. Massah never told us nothing 'bout no freedom for us. He never read us the paper – nobody did. We had already been set free. Ms. Iney was free. She was free when they killed her.

It took me a while after readin' that to get up. All the anger inside me, I wanted to cry for Ms. Iney, but nothin' but a madness came out. I punched the floors until my own hands I couldn't feel no more, and that was when James found me. He came and tapped me on my arm like he was scared of me. Then, after starin' down at the paper for a time, I got up from that floor. He ain't know what was wrong with me as I suppose I looked like I wanted to kill him, so instead of scarin' him worse, I got up and walked out the door, watchin' everybody runnin' 'round grabbin' stuff to use for later, figuring that soon people would be comin' to pay ole dead Massah and his wife a visit sometime and find out they was dead due to what they call a slave rebellion.

I went to the front of the house and shouted. They all stopped, but they smiles never left. I looked up there at some steppin' over that ole Massah Duncan's beat up body while they look over the balcony at me, then, I lifted that paper high, and read it out loud. The smiles got even wider, and the shoutin' even stronger, but soon, the smiles left their faces as they looked around. The faces all turned to fear again, and I ain't like that.

Next thing, I felt something comin' that I didn't feel in a long time. Tears came down my face. They was tears of joy. They came down like strangers, and I hit 'em. They had to move out my way because I didn't know them no more. I didn't know 'em. My people, they saw what happened, and they knew they had to put everything down. There was no need to run, but we all had to get off the land. We had to get off the land and scatter out, and we didn't need papers. We just had to go 'less somebody catch us inside and we all die. If we got caught with somethin' that belong to a white man, they would know, even assume it was them all and not just me that did the killin', and tie it back to us.

"We free. We clearin' the wrong place. We got to split up. Leave them cabins empty. We got 'til mornin'. Nobody better follow me, and I ask you that if somebody say something, that you don't lead 'em my way. We don't know each other no more."

Lil Wani came to hold my hand as I turned to walk out the door. She stood right there with me like I was her own papa, and I felt like she was my own daughter. I felt like they all was my family, but just like I killed for us, I have to leave 'em so that they be safe. I stood there over that Negro overseer body that I killed, and felt bad for him just that fast. Then, as I looked down at Lil Wani to pick her up, her innocent eyes made me feel better about takin' his life. He was our enemy, no matter if he was one of us.

125

"Lil Wani, you can come on with me." As I was talkin', James walked up to me, too. I knew without even sayin' that he was followin' me. The rest knew what they had to do. There was few as young as Lil Wani, so they all did what they had to do. As for us, we walked away. James already had food all in his pockets and he ran back in the house and got some more, and then we headed off. We headed off into Freedom…the Freedom that I took for us that Duncan hid. I figured God let me find it. Through all the blood and all, He let me find it, and we was finally free. I just didn't know the road wasn't gonna be easy.

We had another fight. We had a big one. It lasted long, real long. Times when we ain't had nothin' to eat or drink, no where to sleep but next to each other and the wet ground in the mornin' and the dry one at night. What we built, the whites who owned the laws, kept movin' it, sayin' it wasn't our land. We had a time. We had a time, but we made it, and they never caught me for killin' Massah and them. Nobody told on me 'cause I'd done killed the turnin' one before we split up. I took Lil Wani as my own daughter on paper and even James as my nephew, and I even got a wife later, and we both teach her, her and my own blood boy Oseen Jr., and they got to feel freedom in laughter but pain too still yet. Still yet, that pain kept comin', but before I died, I swore to 'em this here thing – Freedom pain was always better to have than slave pain. If they got to choose, they better choose the free kind 'cause that one be they own choice.

Now look here, as I sleep under this here ground, I heard them fight for their kind of Freedom as the years went by. They never forgot about us, none of our children. They took our pain and our agony and sent it into the ears of God even a hundred some odd years later. I still hear my grands and great grands, and they make me proud. They sing that song there, the one that stomp across all the ground while they walk. It's that song that go "'Fore they just let somebody turn 'em 'round, they gonna march" even farther into the land of –

FREEDOM.

That's what we call our children, our descendants.
We in these here graves, we call 'em Freedom.

Freedom, don't forget about us.

From Author to Reader

Thank you for reading **The Day I Met Freedom**. If you enjoyed, please leave a review and tell a friend. You are appreciated.

Mirika Mayo Cornelius
mirikacornelius.com

Now read an excerpt from the novel

CURSE THE COTTON

CHAPTER 1

"It's time to eat now, y'all, so come on. Day done broke, and the sun won't get any cooler by the minute. You need to get this water out this here bucket, and swallow down some of these nuts, bread, and eggs so we can get in them fields 'fore the sun starts settin' the back way."

Shelone had grown into a woman on the Marksman plantation which was one of the plantations closest to the coast. Mr. Marksman had so much land that he would buy and sell off his slaves as fast as he got them most of the time, just to keep the strongest and fastest hands to himself. As far as Shelone, he'd never traded her off, her nor her children. In order to keep it that way, she trained her children to get up before anyone else, and many times hit the fields before the sun came up. Shelone even gave birth in the fields. After she cleaned up, she made it a point to prove that she could bring in just as much in as the rest, just her and her other three children. She would allow the elderly midwife, who did everything from caring for the young to the older sick, clean and tend to her newborn. Shelone trusted her and would go to breastfeed her baby every hour or so while picking cotton. As a matter of fact, she was who delivered her other three children, kept them healthy and strong with things she learned from her homeland, passed on from her mother. The midwife knew more than any of them about life, and it was easier to trust an old lady who made it through than a young one who hadn't made it through to old age yet.

Back to Mr. Marksman, he made most of his money on cotton and crops. Being that he was close to plenty water, he had good ground for growing. He never had a time when his crops were bad or his cotton wouldn't grow. Every week, he would line his slaves up and watch how they walked, ran, stooped, and stretched. If he saw one thing wrong, he would try his best to sell them off. The slaves learned to ignore their pain, especially the slaves with families. As far as Shelone, she learned to breathe with her pains, and she had many. Her back would ache her constantly, but she never let anyone know. It was only at night that she would cry and moan after her children were asleep. Sometimes, she would take some greens, mainly cabbage if it was available, from the garden during the day, not to eat, but wet in a bucket so that she could wrap herself in them at night. It was the cool leaves mixed with the cold water from the lake that would sooth her neck and back at night. No one would ever know she was in constant pain, and it was that pain that she was willing to endure to not be sold away from her children.

"Yessum," answered her six year old son who was the oldest. After him came five year old girl twins and then there was her baby who was only six months old.

"Here, and take that to your sisters, Cosah, and you head out there first. I checked. Bigun is already out there pickin', and he knows you're coming. Mr. Marksman is still sleepin', so be quiet, and that way, we'll have most of what we need picked. Go on now, and don't you eat a drop of that slop they send to us to eat. My momma ain't eat it and we ain't either. Eat what we make. No tellin' what's in that food from the big house unless Sammy Joe is in there cooking it, but he's not so you ain't eatin' it, you hear me, Cosah?"

"Yes, ma'am," he stated, shoving the food in his mouth and drinking from a half bucket of water. Cosah had a healthy appetite, and generally when it was the overseers time to take a break, he would sneak off to a scupadine vine and eat until he was full, then slither back into the fields unnoticed because he was still small. He would bring back as much as he could for everyone else in his shirt and drop them in a line along the ground in between the rows of cotton so that everyone could get a taste. Cosah was the fastest boy on the plantation and the most inconspicuous. His innocent appearance matched the innocence of his personality, and where Mr. Marksman made it wrong to go off the land during work time, he didn't understand that growing children needed to eat just as much as his white children. Mr. Marksman's children, all three of them, had something in their mouths every hour, and they never shared with anyone, even though they had plenty. It wasn't proper, according to their mother, Sarah, to share with the Negroes or the Negro children. She would let them play together sometimes, but the children dared not touch Mrs. Marksman's children's food, no matter how long her children wanted to play. Shelone would always hope that they would go inside and stay away from her children because the older they got, the more risk it was for her children to play with the whites. Too much could go wrong. With tempers and accidents, it would be Shelone's children to get in trouble, and possibly even sold away. That was why Shelone would always pray that Jesus be with her offspring, whether they were with or without her, but most favorably with her. What made matters even worse was that Mrs. Marksman was pregnant with another one that was due any day, and her attitude was fiercer than a lioness'.

The shack Shelone and her children lived in was the size of one small bedroom in what was called the big house, or *massah's* house. There wasn't a wooden floor inside any of the shacks in the slave quarters at all, but Shelone had one of the bigger in size due to someone who'd given it to them after all her children were sold. It was what they did…watch out for one another for the most part and minus a couple that would hang onto Mr. Marksman's ankles believing that it made them more special than any other African descendant on the plantation. Sure, there were what were called house negroes that worked in the house and what they called field negroes who worked in the fields, but not all house negroes were the turncoat kind either. Most of them kept their heads, or senses, about them, some even tried to kill the *massahs* more often than not. The only reason most would fail was because of that turncoat Negro that thought his slave life under the white man was better than the free life with Negroes. Shelone's mother and father taught her better than that. Freedom anyway it came was always better than being somebody's slave. She had her hopes for it one day.

"Baby girls, Seena and Sadie, get up, wash up your face and head out there behind your brother. I'm gonna give suck to baby brother here, sweethearts, and I'll meet you out there as soon as I drop Abraham off to Lady Rose. Come give me kiss, okay? I love all of you, and watch out for each other. Those snakes are out. Have a switch with you. Break some off the trees out yonder. Stomp that ground hard, you hear?" she whispered firmly and lovingly to her girls.

Shelone reminded them every morning of what to do as if the instructions were brand new. Every night she did the same thing. Absolutely no one shut their eyes without praying to the Lord Jesus, and no one went to bed without reciting their family all the way back to three generations, just in case they ran into someone down the line who was kin, or a relative. She loved them as a mother should, but had to be firmer on them than her heart sometimes desired due to the way she knew they would be treated if they showed any signs of weakness, intelligence, or honor. Those were the three things that she monitored on them constantly. They were only allowed to show who they truly were inside the shack, and they had to do so quietly.

"Yes ma'am, we hear. Love you too, mama," they responded, and after they ate their food and drank down their water, the twins kissed their mother and left behind their big brother. Shelone hated to send them out there as working hands, but she knew what was required to stay put and stay alive, and they needed to be the best. Part of being the best was being the fastest, so she started them young, just like her parents did her. She couldn't even remember the first day she was out in the fields, but she knew that was where she stayed. She held back her tears as she watched all three of them run down to Bigun in the vast rows of cotton. Then she turned to view her youngest child, yearning for the day that she might not have to give him a future like her present and past.

"Jesus, help us." Shelone's back was in major pain, but it never stopped her from lifting her baby. If she could bend and lift for Mr. Marksman, only Jesus himself would keep her from lifting and caring for Abraham. She became the children's only parent when their father died in the river trying to get away from a false accusation. Instead of being strung up to a tree for what everyone saw a white man do, he opted to drown with the fish carrying him off.

His name was Marcus, and he was never a good swimmer. Every slave on the plantation could swim better than him, so it was ironic how the one who couldn't swim would choose that way to die. He knew he was going to die as soon as he stepped in the water because the lake was vast and deep. He'd been inside the lake many times, but it was on that humid, darkening night that he took his last breath after only reaching midway in the waters. Before the water stopped troubling, he shouted out "Freedom!" Then, he was gone.

Shelone's knees, on that particular day, dug inside the dirt so deeply from her holding all three of her older children back from weeping behind their father. They knew what was going on because before Marcus fled, he told Cosah to grow up strong and not to let anyone take his life from him. As soon as those words departed Marcus' mouth, Shelone knew that he was going to die escaping, and it wasn't going to be by the hands of any of the white men.

The fear struck Shelone like a whip, and she fell upon her husband, but she didn't beg him not to go. She only wept, needing him to flee as fast as he could because even deep down in her own soul, she knew that his chosen death was best for him than being strung up on a tree, cut apart, shot down, or even set on fire. She knew that if he didn't get away, Cosah would have to see his father lynched with his own eyes, and a grave fear would set in that would destroy him forever. Cosah saw his father as the strongest man alive, and he clung to his every word. Therefore, as Shelone held on to her children awaiting word on their father after he fled, she already had her story for them prepared. She would tell Cosah, Seena and Sadie that he ran away…to freedom. They would never know the truth. She cried in the fields for one week while her children became happy as a result of her telling them that he got away and they would see him again someday. The other slaves who knew of her lie stuck to her version of the story while they mourned the loss of a brother and true friend.

Needless to say, Shelone would have to raise her youngest without him ever remembering who his father was. Mr. Marksman didn't care about the children's father dying. He only replaced Marcus' hands with another while Bigun continued to train Cosah how to be a strong man. Shelone was grateful.

After feeding baby Abraham all he could suck from her breast, she quickly took him to Lady Rose.

She was a short woman and quite stocky in the face, like her cheeks had muscles in them instead of meat. Her chin jutted out from her face like a boot, and her face was covered in moles. Some of the smaller children when they were bought to come and work on Mr. Marksman's plantation were afraid of her on sight because they'd never seen such an old woman that looked like she did. After being around on the plantation and having Lady Rose tend to them when they were sick and ailing, they would become very fond of her, even to the point where some would call her mother…since they'd parted from their own mothers by force.

"How you doing there, Lady Rose? Abraham ready here now. I got him filled up, and I'll be back soon to get him some more milk in him. Just let me know like normal when he starts cryin' out…I'll see your head scarf from the door."

"Gone out there, chile, 'fore you can get back. I can tend to this child. I mashed up some good old fruits and berries and mixed it all up 'til it be thin as water for this here youngster till you can return. I

141

keeps it mashed. It won't even hurt him. Now, go on. Abraham gone be fine as he always is," she sighed, taking baby Abraham and sitting him next to the two other babies that were inside her slave cabin. There was a mother already inside feeding her newborn and hadn't yet returned to the fields since she gave birth because she nearly died doing it. It was Mr. Marksman's rule that no more than two weeks could pass for a woman to give birth and get back to work, and if she was feeling good, in a shorter time than that. Just because any Negro woman had a child never meant that Mr. Marksman would let her have any rest. There were some plantations that Shelone heard about that were easier going on the pregnant Negro women, but Mr. Marksman's plantation was hard on everyone. He treated his slaves like animals, worse than the stray dogs he fed from out of the woods. He would look straight through them, almost like he saw emptiness inside their bodies, like they had no souls at all.

When Shelone looked into the lady's eyes, she saw all the fear in the world of losing her child which caused her to hurry on out with her own children.

"Alright, Lady Rose. Thank you, now. Thank ya."

"That's what I do, chile. It's why God done put me here, I reckon," she stated softly to herself while she propped the shack's wooden door open to allow the cooler morning breeze to come in before the sun scorched anything that was on the ground later in the day.

As Shelone rushed off, her long skirt dragged the ground while she placed her straw wide brim hat she made for herself atop her head. The sweat already started pouring down her face, but before she got started, she went to tie a sheet on the end of a strong tree branch, just in case Lady Rose needed to bring Abraham out to the fields for her. It was there that she would let him swing, under the shade of the leaves, while she worked if she ever needed to do so.

Bigun had already picked half the row by the time Shelone walked up next to him while she peeked back at her children on the other row behind her.

"Thank you, Bigun. You've been a help to us, you know," she stated having already put her first palm full of cotton inside the sack that was around her shoulders. "I mean, you don't have to wake up like you do the way Marcus…"

Bigun sighed which made her cease from speaking. "Don't mention that again to me, Shelone. A man is supposed to do it for his friend, if they be truly friends. If I had mine with me, I would want somebody willin' to do the same for my boys…and girls, too."

An uneasiness had settled in between them, and it wasn't the first time the air between them wasn't quite right. It seemed like each time they met up after Marcus died, the heaviness between them worsened. They hadn't spoken about Marcus much, so the discussion was burdening. The more Shelone needed to talk to Bigun about it, the less he spoke. She knew that if she would have said one more thing about Marcus while in the fields, he would pick up and go to the other row with the children who picked just as fast and well as she did which would leave her with most of the picking. Therefore, she remained quiet about her deceased husband so that they could have their share of cotton picked early enough to make Mr. Marksman satisfied.

"You plan on going out to Alligator River tonight?" she asked, placing a light smile on her face. "I heard that once the curtain comes good across the sky and only the stars can be seen and heard that Junepea plans on catching a big one."

"With his little self," Bigun laughed. "Them alligators be twice his size, near 'bout three times to four, but where he gets the might from to tackle them beasts and then cook 'em and eat 'em, I just don't know. But yeah, I'm gonna be there alright. Yes, I will. Ain't had a piece of alligator meat in Lord knows how long," he continued with a big smile on his face as she pushed the cotton down into the bag. "Are you goin'?"

"Now you know I can't go out there and watch Junepea tonight," she responded with a sigh and wiping her forehead. The sun wasn't even high in the sky yet, and Shelone's body was nearly drenched. The humidity hovered over the land like a burning furnace.

"You got that brand new baby boy."

"You know I do," she laughed.

"I can still take Cosah for you, so he can learn…"

She reached over and slapped him on the arm. "Learn him what, Bigun? Don't you go hurtin' my child now!"

He laughed his hardest, and she slapped him on the arm once again, causing him to reach for her hand, not forcefully, but gently. Bigun's laughter faded as he brought her hand down and lowered his gaze toward her deep, brown eyes, and she quickly snatched her hand back, looked back at her children who still had their heads down concentrating on not getting cut up by the cotton bristles, and then pretended that Bigun never gave her such a tender look or touch.

Disturbed and overtaken by guilt, Shelone forced her recovery from what she considered an uncomfortable moment in the fields, shoved her eyes back down to the rows of white fluff beneath her and started to yank once again. Her eyes filled with tears as she watched Bigun from her periphery continue to stare at her without moving his feet one inch, preventing her from moving beyond him on the same path. Therefore, as he stared at her, increasing the tension between them, Shelone walked around him and continued down the row of cotton. Bigun followed her with his eyes, but finally, after noticing Cosah look up, he began picking cotton again as well.

"I see how he looks at you out there in them fields there, Shelone, and he right fine a man and all," spoke a slim, young, bronze-toned lady that was named Lily. "Bigun…he likes you, alright…"

"I don't want to talk about that right now, Lily. You go starting foolish talking like that…"

"Well, it's true. He's always looking at you, and since Marcus done left, I feel like you shouldn't look toward them waters no more because they're not gonna vomit him up. He's on with God above now, and…"

Shelone interrupted again, except more hostile than before. "I said be quiet, Lily. You got no right to tell me where I need to look before I rest my head at night. Bigun is good to Cosah and the rest of my children. He was Marcus' best friend out here, and I believe Bigun, if he wasn't sent off at the time, would have died right along with Marcus himself."

"And what that got to do with him making eyes at you now, Shelone?" Lily stressed, standing from the grassy meadow to look whom she saw as a confused friend in the face. "Death done freed you up."

"I got children! I got Cosah! He believes his daddy is alive, and you know that," she exclaimed,

148

tossing loose grass as Lily's feet. "Everybody knows that."

"Well, it's time you change that, now ain't it? You know Cosah growing up right along with the rest of them, and one day, he's gonna go looking and asking more and more, until finally, somebody tells him the hard truth. Do you want that, huh?"

Shelone kept quiet, and the only reason she kept quiet while giving suck to baby Abraham was because she'd never thought about the truth getting out to Cosah and the twins. The fact was, she wanted the truth to die so quickly that everyone's tongue wouldn't feel so latched up from what happened a little over six months ago. Shelone always believed that time was the only thing on her side besides Jesus.

"I don't want that, Lily, and you know I don't, but," she answered while placing Abraham on her other breast to feed. "Bigun is an alright gentleman to me and my children. I just can't waltz around here with him. It's too much for me right now. 'Sides that, I see him as a brother," she turned her head away from Lily as she spoke. "Nothing more and not much less."

"Not much, huh?"

"You heard me."

"Well, you best to hurry up 'fore he sets his eyes on somebody else with no children around here. Looks like to me, he must really like you if he willin' to do all he doin' for you for nothing."

"It's for Marcus," Shelone stated quietly. "Just for him is all. Nothing to do with me." She stood up in front of Lily. "There go Mr. Marksman there coming down from the big house. Let me get my baby back in there to Lady Rose. The less he sees my baby, the less likely it is Abraham will be leaving me." She glanced up and saw that her other children positioned their heads lower to the cotton like she taught them to do because it appeared like they were working harder and faster than if they heads were high. "Lily, go 'head and take them these berries and bread out there. I had my fill, and tell them to eat them all, 'specially Seena and Sadie. They tend to eat only what they want and give the rest to Cosah who is always there waitin'. Boy eats so much, I don't know if I can feed him good out here."

Lily laughed and took the berries and bread to Shelone's children as Shelone made her way back to Lady Rose's shack. On the way back, she turned to her right toward Mr. Marksman's balcony and noticed Mrs. Sarah rubbing her stomach while watching her walk toward her destination. Immediately, their eyes met, causing Shelone to hug her baby tighter and stand stronger, crushing the pain of her backside with her dominating will power. Quickly, her eyes turned from Mrs. Sarah, and she began praying, hoping that she wouldn't be called over to the house for anything. All Shelone wanted to do was stay out of sight, and each time she made eye contact with Mrs. Sarah, she cringed knowing that it was many times her own doing that Mr. Marksman would do away with certain slaves.

It was back during the summer, a summer that happened three years back, and every slave who was on the plantation never forgot it. Mrs. Sarah was walking through the yards, something that she rarely did, so when she did it, everybody outside and inside noticed. It was only when her husband left the premises that she would walk outside and off from the home where a small row of shacks were off some distance from the big house and beyond the other shacks. Even though everyone would watch her most times, it was Shelone who saw it all that particular day, and she'd wished she'd never seen it at all.

There was a man who was brought onto the plantation, sold to Mr. Marksman for plenty money. The word was that he was one of the strongest, if not the strongest, Negro men brought from up north after having escaped. He'd hurt a white man in the process of them capturing him, but because he was so fit, they tied up and whipped him sore until he couldn't stand up straight because they didn't want to lose such a strong hand. On top of that, the money that Mr. Marksman paid for him was worth more than what he'd done to that white man. If Mr. Marksman wanted him alive and well, that was the way they were to deliver him. The only thing was that they had to let him heal first, and he healed just as well as he looked before they beat him.

When he first got to Mr. Marksman's plantation, he didn't talk, but they already knew his name. Everyone knew him as Isaac Walters, but he didn't really care what anyone called him because he knew that Isaac Walters wasn't his real name. He'd changed it when he got up north, and never revealed his real name to anyone. That truth got out when he fell in love with a girl named Tanna who was also on the land...until Mrs. Sarah came along.

Isaac lived in his own hut with his own set of work to do for Mr. Marksman. He would join some of the other men to work the farm and handle the horses and build and fix items needed to be repaired all the time. In doing so, Mrs. Sarah would see him all the time because he spent much time walking to and from the big house. Sometimes, she would call him to help her with things that the other house Negroes could have helped her with, and Isaac always obliged. She would peep out of her window, and if she could, interrupt his meeting with Tanna whenever they were spending time. Mr. Marksman knew nothing about it, and no one dare said a word even though everyone knew Mrs. Sarah was a heated dog for Isaac. They knew Mr. Marksman would kill him dead…two times if he had to do so…and he was an innocent man. It was his wife who showed up at his shack's door one day, and that was the day she lost her mind.

"Mrs. Sarah?" Isaac asked, confused as he opened his front door. His shirt was off, and because he stood half naked in front of Mr. Marksman's wife, he shut the door, but she caught it with the palm of her hand. He didn't dare shove her out. Instead, he left the doorway to go and put on his work shirt believing that she needed some help in the early hours of the morning. Before he turned back to face her, she was already inside, having undressed the top half and breathing like an asthmatic.

"If even you don't want me, Isaac…a full grown Negro man like yourself… then I got no chance of keeping my husband happy, now do I?" she boldly spoke in her deeply southern accent to an unshaken Isaac. He'd been in that position before because he was a handsome man. All women loved to look at him, including the married ones, because they would always look down when he passed by as if they didn't see him. Yes, all the women loved him, including the white ones, whether they admitted it or not. Mrs. Sarah was no exception.

"There's not a man on this earth wouldn't want you, Mrs. Sarah," he responded, lying in order to make her feel good because he knew she didn't want to know his truth. His truth was that he wouldn't dare touch a white woman if they were the only ladies on the earth. That came with a death sentence whether they were single or married, so as he stood there looking at her undress while staring back at him, he walked past her and out of his front door. He knew he had to run.

It wasn't long before the screams of Mrs. Sarah's broken pride came through the wooden walls of Isaac's shack, and he heard them loud and clear as he ran his fastest toward Tanna's shack. He woke her up and kissed her passionately.

"Just know I didn't do it. I ain't touch her. Look at me, Tanna. Smell me," he said, placing her body against his in order to prove that he smelled like no one else but himself. "I got to run. The sun is almost up."

Tanna knew exactly what and who he was talking about, and as they stood still in each other's arms, she heard Mrs. Sarah's screams coming through the walls. Her breathing stopped, and she raised her eyes to Isaac's as he caressed the back of her head. Then, he tenderly kissed the tears that ran down her cheeks before letting her loose. Finally, he began to walk out of the door, but Tanna grabbed his arm.

"I'm running, too." Her eyes were convinced that she belonged with Isaac, and even if they weren't yet married, she felt it was 'til death. She loved him just like she loved her own soul, and she also knew he told the truth about not doing anything to Mrs. Sarah...because he'd never done anything with her. It was all pure love.

For the first time, Isaac shoved her back, and she nearly fell against the opposite wall. However, she stood up straight, strong and as tall as she could, put on her shoes and reminded him of why he loved her so.

"I said, I'm coming! If you run faster than me, I'll find you, but I'm not staying here no more if you ain't, Isaac. Ain't no violence against me gonna keep me from you 'cause you don't scare me, and it ain't in you to hurt me. I'm coming!"

That was all it took for Isaac to give up. "Then I'll stay. I'm not alive right now so that I can see you die, so I'll stay."

Tanna ran over to him and gripped his shirt like it was going to be the last time she would see him. "We're runnin', Isaac, and I won't see you die. I'll go kill her myself for even thinking to set you up. Now, we either run together and try to make it, or we die. Either way, we die, because you won't go alone." She, then, dropped his shirt. "I'm already dead." Her tears dried up and she looked around her desperately small shack with one hole for a window.

"We already dead. Out there," she continued softly, "we can at least be free for a time. A short time, but a time."

It took no time for Isaac to take her by the hand. They both ran off as the echoes of Mrs. Sarah's screams pounded their eardrums in plans for the hanging of Isaac. As they ran, they passed their fellow slaves walking outside and rushing toward Isaac's shack where they heard the screaming, and without even asking a question, they already knew what was going on because they'd seen Mrs. Sarah's eyes on Isaac the whole time he'd been on the plantation. Some of them waved good-bye as they did their natural duty – go and see about Mrs. Sarah as she screamed. Her screaming meant nothing more than a hanging – nothing more and nothing less.

It was Shelone who watched the whole lie take place from the back of her shack. She'd gotten up early as usual to wash out some of her undergarments that they were only allowed three of per year, and after she watched Mrs. Sarah walk into Isaac's shack and Isaac walk back out, she dropped to the ground in tears because she knew what was coming. Mrs. Sarah's screams got louder and louder, so loud until Shelone fearfully covered her ears, but when she looked up, there was a slight pause to her screams because Mrs. Sarah's eyes looked directly at her. That was when Shelone knew that death would come her way if she'd ever opened her mouth.

Shelone got off the ground and ran the opposite way, back into her shack and cuddled her children. She knew that screaming was a lie just like Mrs. Sarah knew she was caught. It didn't matter for Isaac if Mrs. Sarah was caught in a lie or not, though. When the whites finally caught up to Isaac and Tanna, they were both killed dead and dragged back through the plantation tied to the back of the horse drawn carriage. The ropes were cut and their necks dropped to the ground. It was the slaves that carried them off and buried them near the waterside. Shelone never came outside because she knew Mrs. Sarah would have been watching her…and her kids. Since then, she'd never stopped watching.

**

When she made it back to Lady Rose's shack, she went directly in and sat down. She began to rock baby Abraham and pray while Lady Rose looked on.

"Let go of him, chile," Lady Rose advised her. "You need to get to work. Them prayers you sending up will be with him wherever you are and wherever he is, but Mr. Marksman needs to see you in them fields yonder, now don't he? Let him lose," she continued, but Shelone snatched her arms away from Lady Rose as she reached for Abraham. There was no harm done to Lady Rose's heart, however, because she understood. All of her children were taken from her at a young age, so the way Shelone held her child in her arms like it was going to be the last time she was going to see him only reminded Lady Rose of the pain she'd learned to walk around with for years. The weight of it all didn't make her fall over, but it made her stand stronger to watch all the other children in place of her own.

"God will give baby Abraham here good hands, to feel around for himself as he learns the way. He will also give him good hands around him to help him along the way so he can make it if'n we drop dead around him."

Shelone shot a fearful glance at Lady Rose, but then calmed down quickly as she allowed the words to marinate in her mind. Finally, she handed Abraham over.

"We gone leave here on our own or by them there whites, but either way, we got to be strong to teach our children how to be just as strong after we leave. You hear me?" She looked sternly at Shelone. "Can't teach that by talkin' neither. Got to teach 'em by doing it and lettin' 'em see." She turned to walk away with Abraham. "God gonna judge them whites for all they done, and when He do, you get to stand back and watch with your hands as clean as the waters. We gonna make it."

Lady Rose always knew what to say, and she was right. She was older than everyone, but they all saw how she made it through. That perseverance made it easier on everyone because it was evidence to their hope. As she watched Lady Rose lay her baby boy down, she allowed all hopeless thoughts to leave her mind, and when she stepped back outside the door, only glancing quickly to her left, Mrs. Sarah was gone.

CHAPTER 2

The night came in peacefully after a full day of picking cotton. There were so many bags full that when they all piled together, they could hide about twenty slaves for escaping if need be. Along with all that cotton came sore muscles and fingers that had already become numb to the vicious nature of the bristles that attacked like thorns. It seemed like cotton was the most dangerous thing in the world coming up from the ground. It never looked like it, but if it was touched the wrong way, it would lay a nasty wound across a person's hand. It was the most deceitful plant that ever came up other than a rose. Those bristles were disguised so well by the pretty white fluff that it started a tale amongst the slaves that likened the cotton plant to the blood line of the white man. If you got to the core of it, there wasn't nothing but evil. Many slaves never met a good white person down south because the only good person to them would be the person to set them free. There was none of those willing to do so.

After putting Abraham down to sleep along with the twins and Cosah, Shelone walked outside her shack and before she could turn her head to the side, she heard Lady Rose calling her name.

"Yes ma'am, I'm here. What you doing out so late? You alright?" Shelone knew Lady Rose was normally asleep already when nightfall set in good, so this was out of the ordinary for her. "Come on and have a seat over here."

"I want you to go to that alligator catching tonight."

"Why, Lady Rose? I got my children," Shelone asked confused while placing a pillow underneath Lady Rose's feet as she sat down.

"Just gone out there. I'm gonna be here for you, and you know I give my life for any of y'all out'chere. You need to go. Get some life back inside you before your life is all over. Go on now, and I'm not tellin' you any extra now."

"Okay, Lady Rose," she replied with a big smile on her face. It had been a while since she was able to go anywhere since Abraham was born, and she didn't want to seem too ready to get out and go to the river even though she was elated. Therefore, she ran back inside, gave all four of her children kisses on the cheeks, poured some food in a bowl for Abraham, and left. "I'll be back shortly, Lady Rose, and thank you! The food…"

"I brought my own for the baby, now go on. You know round 'bout what time I'll be needin' ya. I reckon I'll go in and get me some sleep, too."

"I won't be long. Thank you," Shelone shouted as she darted off. Nighttime was a whole other world for her because she didn't have to face the realities of the day. Everything her and her friends did at night was hidden from Mr. Marksman, and that was just how she and the others liked it.

Every time there was a get together, there were appointed people to stay back just in case they needed to get back fast. There was a call, a distinct signal that would echo through the woods, and it would pass along for everyone to get back to their cabins fast. They always had a plan because they always needed one, or even a couple. It was a language that only the slaves knew, and it wasn't ever supposed to be shared to the whites. It was never relayed like that, but always automatically understood. If their language was ever found out, they would change it quickly, leaving the whites confused whenever they became educated on it.

By the time Shelone got to what they renamed Alligator River, everyone was already sitting on top of a long, fallen tree that had been there for years. The tree was huge, and the trunk alone sat a good twenty people, some on top of it and some to rest their back against it, as they watched Junepea, who wasn't but the size of a rail, wrestle an alligator in the pitch black of night.

Before Shelone was within ten feet of the tree where she would take a seat with everyone else, someone tapped her on the shoulder and then moved a hand to the side of her waist. Shelone was startled and swiftly turned around to see no one else but Bigun standing behind her.

"You walked right by me."

"I did?"

"I was right there at the tree," he answered, pointing at his previous location. "Thought you wasn't coming out here for this alligator hunt. I'm just out here so I can try to save Junepea from them jaws yonder," he joked.

"Amen, because he shole will need it, won't he?" she laughed. "You gonna help him skin it, Bigun?" she asked, turning back around to face the waters, feeling more relaxed since she had someone...a male...to talk to and laugh with. She missed having that since she became a widow.

"Clance."

Shelone turned back to face him, not understanding what he'd just stated, but before she asked him again, he repeated himself.

"It's Clance. Clance...are you gonna help him skin it?" He stared intimately back at Shelone, and she felt every part of his gaze take over her lonely

167

soul. They'd never been alone in this manner before, and no one even knew they were there although they were that close to the event. Deep down inside the most secret parts of her heart, she wanted it to stay that way, which was why when Clance reached for her hand, she accepted it. They both walked in the opposite direction, away from Alligator River.

There was a smaller stream located in the direction where they were headed, where fresh food always growing and hidden away from Mr. Marksman's eyesight. They stopped walking when they got a small distance from the stream, and Shelone took her hand from Clance's warm touch. Unhappy with her distance, he walked in front of her, obviously unable to hold back what he had to say because it was like something came over him and was trying to push the words out until he finally said it.

"I love you, Shelone."

She stood there before him, unable to return any words, and every piece of her flesh became weak, revealing its wounds in tears that she struggled to hold back. Shelone knew very well why she cried. It was because she didn't know how to tell him any of her truths back. Shame took over her at the thought, and when she turned to walk away, he called her once again.

"Shelone, please. Don't leave me here without you. Life is hard enough as it is, and I need you here with me, Shelone. Don't walk away. I'm tryin'."

His pleas broke through to Shelone's heart quickly because she'd never heard him beg a soul before. It wasn't fit for a Negro man to beg. It was shameful, and the only time she'd heard it was when a Negro man was about to lose his life, and even then, most of them would rather have died than to send a tear drop next to their *massah's* feet. If they lived after begging, they were never the same for a while. Shelone had only seen begging break a man, and if he did it, he was speaking from his heart, and it should be heard. She stopped in her tracks because she needed to face her truth as well.

When she turned back around, she wiped the tears from her eyes and watched as he inhaled, his strong chest hoping for the best from her and not the worst. She'd fooled herself for so long that Clance was only doing what a good man would do after Marcus passed. Something changed between them in that time, and they both knew it.

Clance walked toward her, and Shelone met him halfway. For the first time ever, Shelone yearned to tell a man other than Marcus, this particular man, that she loved him, too, as she choked back the tears that were rooted in Marcus' memory. She felt ashamed, but as Clance began to cry as well, she knew then that he felt the same way. They both felt like they were doing wrong, but they also felt that they had to be with each other somehow.

Clance reached out and touched her face as she comforted herself into the palm of his hand. Her eyes shut, but when she felt the warmth of his presence come near her face and his lips soothe hers, she refused to open them, and kissed him back. She kissed him back until the memory of Marcus refused to disturb her again after she permitted herself to open up and take in her new comfort.

As she kissed him, she softly rubbed the tears away from his face with her fingertips, and as she leaned into his pain at the same time he caressed the wounded places of her heart, she gave herself over to him to fall in love. She was tired of fighting. Her whole world was a struggle, and for once, she needed something to be easy. Clance moved away from her lips and developed a deep connection with her eyes.

"Can you love me back, Shelone?" He held her hand tightly, afraid to let her go, terrified of the rejection that he knew could come. Shelone saw the desperation in his eyes, and she felt the sense of loss creeping up on her if he were to ever leave her life. She knew she had to tell him. She knew she could finally tell him.

"I love you, Clance…very much. I'm sorry…"

"Don't be," he interrupted softly, "and don't cry anymore. Don't cry anymore. We don't have to cry…not anymore." He cradled her body as she embraced him, and they both soothed each others' pains and desires while they only faintly heard the capture of an alligator by little Junepea. Soon, they decided to move toward the commotion.

"Junepea, Junepea, man, you be something else, I tell you," one of the onlookers shouted as he slapped his leg with a full grin. Everyone was just as happy as he was as Junepea laid on top of the animal and wrapped his jaws with a rope as tightly as he could while the other men piled on top of the animal to keep it still.

The alligator he caught at this particular time wasn't as big as the last one, but it was big enough to feed everyone on the plantation. After he tied the mouth together everyone walked around it, felt it and even got on top of it before Junepea and two other men killed it and started to skin it while seated in front of a small fire that added extra light where the moon and stars didn't.

Everyone brought their sacks for the meat, and as Clance walked up behind the crowd along with

Shelone, he noticed her hesitation, understood it, and stalled his gait. "It don't have to be now."

Shelone stared at everyone, and then glanced beyond them to a place that wasn't within her line a vision to the lake where Marcus died. Then, she took a deep breath, slid her fingers in between Clance's, while continuing to stare forward, knowing all the things she had to make right with her children and the lie that she told. Then, she responded, "I can." She then looked up at the man that stood over her, hardly as domineering as his build fabricated him to be. Shelone knew she was safe and in the care of the kindest man since Marcus' death, and it was those qualities about him that gave her the strength to proceed into the crowd.

As Junepea and the others were nearly finished slicing the skin off the alligator and had already started to take the legs off before cutting it down the middle, a couple of people already noticed the togetherness of Shelone and who they still called Bigun. She watched as one lady's hand went up across her face as her other hand tapped the shoulder of the woman in front of her. When the tapped lady turned around and saw Shelone and Bigun holding hands, there was a pause as her eyes lit up. It was Lily, and she was overjoyed.

"Look! Look! Come here and look, y'all!" Immediately, she ran towards a smiling Shelone and a proud Bigun, scooting herself right in between them, causing their hands to break apart. Then, she pulled Shelone over to the side of a tree as the other ladies followed behind, giggling and amazed to see her and Bigun together how they were. When Shelone looked back, some of the men had already begun lightly punching Bigun on the shoulder and laughing with him about what was going on.

"So tell us, Shelone," the ladies squealed as they all piled around her in a circle, happy that she'd finally moved forward into what they'd already known should've happened a while ago.

"I was on the way up here with y'all, and he pulled me over to the side…and told me he loved me!" Shelone could barely contain her excitement and tears started to fall down her cheeks. Lily saw them flowing, and she reached over and wiped them off of her face like a mother would a child. Then, she held on to Shelone's hands.

"Didn't I tell you that man loved you, huh? I told you everything was gonna be just fine, now didn't I? Ain't nobody crazy 'round here, Shelone. We all saw Bigun and how he watched her, ain't we?" she asked the women who responded positively in laughter and chatter. "If that man want to be with you and your children, let him. Make life ten times easier on you…and us…especially in the winter time!" she laughed thinking about how Shelone used to ask her deceased husband to collect wood to burn for certain close friends.

When Lily said that, she noticed a slight change in Shelone's expression, and quickly moved away from the topic that she knew had reminded her of her deceased husband. She then, latched onto Shelone's hand and said, "Well, come on then! Let's go get some of this alligator meat, so tomorrow we can have it cooked up and ready to eat. How about that now?"

175

"That sounds good to me," Shelone replied, casting the thought of Marcus to the way side once again. She glanced in the direction of the lake where he died once more, and inside her heart, she stated, "I love you."

They all gathered together, Shelone with the ladies and Clance with his friends, back at the edge of the water, and everyone noticed how Clance couldn't keep his eyes off of Shelone for one second. In another hour, everyone was gone, and the two new lovers walked away slowly back to Shelone's shack. When Shelone's small cabin was within sight, Clance stopped and pulled Shelone in closer to him.

There were rows and rows of cotton beside them, just like a white sheet covering the ground. Just the sight of it made them ache which was why they rarely looked that way when the picking was over. They'd rather blind one eye than to wake up day by day having that back breaking work greet them.

"One day soon, Shelone, I want you and the children to come with me."

"Come where, Clance?"

"We're getting out of here."

Shelone paused and dropped his hands, refusing to acknowledge what she considered senseless and useless talk. "Why are you talking like this, and right now?" Frustration took over the night at that moment, and before he even spoke, she'd already turned to walk away, regretting everything that she'd done with him that night. He didn't allow her to go far before he jumped in front of her, blocking her way.

"We got no choice. Freedom is only that far away," he continued, pointing back through the woods. "How long you think we can be together under Mr. Marksman, huh? As soon as I get old or hurt or you don't have children fast enough, I'm gone, and possibly even you too unless he'll keep you on for the children's sake like Lady Rose." He paused as she looked to the ground. "You know I'm tellin' the truth. What we got…like three years 'fore something happen to me or you…or God forbid…"

"Shut up, now!" she answered sharply. "Ain't nothing never gonna happen." She turned her head back to her cabin and then back at him, disgusted by the fact that he was about to speak something against her children. "I hurt, but I work. You know it! Me and my children the best on this land. Now, I'm not gonna put my children at no risk for you or anybody else!"

"And I'm not askin' you to, Shelone! I ain't leavin' here with no plan in place. I'm not talkin' about just runnin' out of here, but I'm talkin' about a plan," he stressed, resting his hands on her shoulders. "Me and Marcus even talked about it."

"What?"

"Yes, we did. 'Fore he died and all that stuff happened at the big house. Yeah we did. He said he had a feeling it was bad times coming, and he was right. Think about it, Shelone. Even if nothing does happen to you, how many whole and together families you see round here. Even your first one already broke apart, so how much time you think we got 'fore Sarah or Mr. Marksman give word to another plantation?"

Shelone didn't answer because she knew he was right. Time was ticking, and she nor her son Cosah was getting any younger. Because he was the oldest and strongest of her children, he would be the first to go. For all she knew, another person could easily come on the land and request Cosah for the right amount of money, and her son would be gone away from her for good. The only thing she'd taught him to do was stay alive and work, but he didn't know how to live without her. That was the one thing that she didn't know if he could do, without losing his mind over to slavery for good which would lead to his death.

"Shelone, hear me, please. I won't go if you don't, but if you will, I'll plan our way out here. Baby Abraham can be gone before us, and …"

"Shhh! Just," she swiped her hand in front of his face diagonally because she didn't want to hear anymore. "Don't talk to me about this anymore. Just let me come to you with a yes or no. Give me time, just some days is all. I have to make sure I can...we can." Then, her eyes finally met his again, only able to see her future inside them, and without him, there was just about nothing left but the cotton and the grave. She would honestly rather die and go to the Lord before all her hope left.

"I love you. I truly do love you, and the first thing I want us to do, all of us to do, is be free. I want it that way, and that's the only reason for me hesitatin' to even be with you, Shelone. I didn't want to tell you, and I was even hoping my feelings about you didn't grow like they did. But it did, and I got no choice but to love you, even more than I love myself. If I try to be free, I need you to be."

"I been just trying to stay alive, Clance, that's all," she silently cried.

"Being alive ain't never been enough. It ain't never been." It was with those words that he took her in his arms and hugged her as tightly as he could, caressing her head that laid against his chest. Then, he kissed her on her forehead, cheek and lips, releasing her to go back home. He watched her as she walked the short distance back before he turned toward his hut.

As soon as Shelone went inside, she fed baby Abraham, kissed her other children, and then slid next to a sleeping Lady Rose to also fall asleep.

If you enjoyed this Curse the Cotton excerpt, enjoy reading it by ordering it in paperback or digital e-book.

Thank you.